GEORGES SIMENON

The Carter of La Providence

Translated by DAVID COWARD

PENGUIN BOOKS

PENGUIN CLASSICS

UK | USA | Canada | Ireland | Australia
India | New Zealand | South Africa

Penguin Books is part of the Penguin Random House group of companies
whose addresses can be found at global.penguinrandomhouse.com.

 Penguin
Random House
UK

First published in French as *Le Charretier de la Providence* by Fayard 1931
This translation first published 2014

015

Copyright 1931 by Georges Simenon Limited
Translation © David Coward, 2014
GEORGES SIMENON ®
MAIGRET ®
All rights reserved

Set in Dante 12.5/15 pt.
Typeset by Palimpsest Book Production Limited, Falkirk, Stirlingshire
Printed and bound in Great Britain by Clays Ltd, Elcograf S.p.A.

ISBN: 978-0-141-39346-9

Contents

1. *Lock 14*

The facts of the case, though meticulously reconstructed, proved precisely nothing – except that the discovery made by the two carters from Dizy made, frankly, no sense at all.

On the Sunday – it was 4 April – it had begun to rain heavily at three in the afternoon.

At that moment, moored in the reach above Lock 14, which marks the junction of the river Marne and the canal, were two motor barges, both heading downstream, a canal boat which was being unloaded and another having its bilges washed out.

Shortly before seven, just as the light was beginning to fade, a tanker-barge, the *Éco-III*, had hooted to signal its arrival and had eased itself into the chamber of the lock.

The lock-keeper had not been best pleased, because he had relatives visiting at the time. He had then waved 'no' to a boat towed by two plodding draught horses which arrived in its wake only minutes later.

He had gone back into his house but had not been there long when the man driving the horse-drawn boat, who he knew, walked in.

'Can I go through? The skipper wants to be at Juvigny for tomorrow night.'

'If you like. But you'll have to manage the gates by yourself.'

The rain was coming down harder and harder. Through his window, the lock-keeper made out the man's stocky figure as he trudged wearily from one gate to the other, driving both horses on before making the mooring ropes fast to the bollards.

The boat rose slowly until it showed above the lock side. It wasn't the barge master standing at the helm but his wife, a large woman from Brussels, with brash blonde hair and a piercing voice.

By 7.20 p.m., the *Providence* was tied up by the Café de la Marine, behind the *Éco-III*. The tow-horses were taken on board. The carter and the skipper headed for the café where other boat men and two pilots from Dizy had already assembled.

At eight o'clock, when it was completely dark, a tug arrived under the lock with four boats in tow.

Its arrival swelled the crowd in the Café de la Marine. Six tables were now occupied. The men from one table called out to the others. The newcomers left puddles of water behind them as they stamped the mud off their boots.

In the room next door, a store lit by an oil-lamp, the women were buying whatever they needed.

The air was heavy. Talk turned to an accident that had happened at Lock 8 and how much of a hold-up this would mean for boats travelling upstream.

At nine o'clock, the wife of the skipper of the *Providence* came looking for her husband and their carter. All three of them then left after saying goodnight to all.

By ten o'clock, the lights had been turned out on most of the boats. The lock-keeper accompanied his relations as far as the main road to Épernay, which crosses the canal two kilometres further on from the lock.

He did not notice anything out of the ordinary. On his way back, he walked past the front of the café. He looked in and was greeted by a pilot.

'Come and have a drink! Man, you're soaked to the skin . . .'

He ordered rum, but did not sit down. Two carters got up, heavy with red wine, eyes shining, and made their way out to the stable adjoining the café, where they slept on straw, next to their horses.

They weren't exactly drunk. But they had had enough to ensure that they would sleep like logs.

There were five horses in the stable, which was lit by a single storm lantern, turned down low.

At four in the morning, one of the carters woke his mate, and both began seeing to their animals. They heard the horses on the *Providence* being led out and harnessed.

At the same time, the landlord of the café got up and lit the lamp in his bedroom on the first floor. He also heard the *Providence* as it got under way.

At 4.30, the diesel engine of the tanker-barge spluttered into life, but the boat did not leave for another quarter of an hour, after its skipper had swallowed a bracing hot toddy in the café which had just opened for business.

He had scarcely left and his boat had not yet got as far as the bridge when the two carters made their discovery.

One of them was leading his horses out to the towpath.

The other was ferreting through the straw looking for his whip when one hand encountered something cold.

Startled, because what he had touched felt like a human face, he fetched his lantern and cast its light on the corpse which was about to bring chaos to Dizy and disrupt life on the canal.

Detective Chief Inspector Maigret of the Flying Squad was running through these facts again, putting them in context.

It was Monday evening. That morning, magistrates from the Épernay prosecutor's office had come out to make the routine inspection of the scene of the crime. The body, after being checked by the people from Criminal Records and examined by police surgeons, had been moved to the mortuary.

It was still raining, a fine, dense, cold rain which had gone on falling without stopping all night and all day.

Shadowy figures came and went around the lock gates, where a barge was rising imperceptibly.

The inspector had been there for an hour and had got no further than familiarizing himself with a world which he was suddenly discovering and about which, when he arrived, he had had only mistaken, confused ideas.

The lock-keeper had told him:

'There was hardly anything in the canal basin: just two motor barges going downstream, one motorized barge heading up, which had gone through the lock in the afternoon, one boat cleaning out its bilges and two panamas. Then the tin tub turned up with four vessels in tow . . .'

In this way did Maigret learn that a 'tin tub' is a tug and a 'panama' a boat without either an engine or its own horses on board, which employs a carter with his own animals for a specified distance, known in the trade as 'hitching a lift'.

When he arrived at Dizy all he'd seen was a narrow canal, three miles from Épernay, and a small village near a stone bridge.

He had had to slog through the mud of the towpath to reach the lock, which was two kilometres from Dizy.

There he had found the lock-keeper's house. It was made of grey stone, with a board that read: 'Office'.

He had walked into the Café de la Marine, which was the only other building in the area.

On his left was a run-down café-bar with brown oil-cloth-covered tables and walls painted half brown and half a dirty yellow.

But it was full of the characteristic odour which marked it out as different from the usual run of country cafés. It smelled of stables, harness, tar, groceries, oil and diesel.

There was a small bell just by the door on the right. Transparent advertisements had been stuck over the glass panels.

Inside was full of stock: oilskins, clogs, canvas clothes, sacks of potatoes, kegs of cooking oil and packing cases containing sugar, dried peas and beans cheek-by-jowl with fresh vegetables and crockery.

There were no customers in sight. The stable was

empty except for the horse which the landlord only saddled up when he went to market, a big grey as friendly as a pet dog. It was not tethered and at intervals would walk around the yard among the chickens.

Everywhere was sodden with rainwater. It was the most striking thing about the place. And the people who passed by were black, gleaming figures who leaned into the rain.

A hundred metres away, a narrow-gauge train shunted backwards and forwards in a siding. The carter had rigged up an umbrella on the back of the miniature engine and he crouched under it, shivering, with shoulders hunched.

A barge hauled by boat hooks slid along the canal bank heading for the lock chamber, from which another was just emerging.

How had the woman got here? And why? That was what had baffled the police at Épernay, the prosecutor's people, the medics and the specialists from Records. Maigret was now turning it over and over in his heavy head.

She had been strangled, that was the first sure fact. Death had occurred on the Sunday evening, probably around 10.30.

And the body had been found in the stable a little after four in the morning.

There was no road anywhere near the lock. There was nothing there to attract anyone not interested in barges and canals. The towpath was too narrow for a car. On the night in question anyone on foot would have had to wade knee deep through the puddles and mud.

It was obvious that the woman belonged to a class where people were more likely to ride in expensive motor-cars and travel by sleeper than walk.

She had been wearing only a beige silk dress and white buckskin shoes designed more for the beach than for city streets.

The dress was creased, but there was no trace of mud on it. Only the toe of the left shoe was wet when she was found.

'Between thirty-eight and forty,' the doctor had said after he'd examined the body.

Her earrings were real pearls worth about 15,000 francs. Her bracelet, a mixture of gold and platinum worked in the very latest style, was more artistic than costly even though it was inscribed with the name of a jeweller in the Place Vendôme.

Her hair was brown, waved and cut very short at the nape of the neck and temples.

The face, contorted by the effects of strangulation, must have been unusually pretty.

No doubt a bit of a tease.

Her manicured, varnished fingernails were dirty.

Her handbag had not been found near her. Police officers from Épernay, Rheims and Paris, armed with a photograph of the body, had been trying all day to establish her identity but without success.

Meanwhile the rain continued to fall with no let-up over the dreary landscape. To left and right, the horizon was bounded by chalk hills streaked with white and black, where at this time of year the vines looked like wooden crosses in a Great War cemetery.

The lock-keeper, recognizable only because he wore a silver braided cap, trudged wearily around the chamber of the lock, in which the water boiled every time he opened the sluices.

And every time a vessel was raised or lowered he told the tale to each new bargee.

Sometimes, after the official papers had been signed, the two of them would hurry off to the Café de la Marine and down a couple or three glasses of rum or a half litre of white wine.

And every time, the lock-keeper would point his chin in the direction of Maigret, who was prowling around with no particular purpose and thus probably made people think he did not know what he was doing.

Which was true. There was nothing normal about the case. There was not even a single witness who could be questioned.

For once the people from the prosecutor's office had interviewed the lock-keeper and spoken to the Waterways Board's civil engineer, they had decided that all the boats were free to go on their way.

The two carters had been the last to leave, around noon, each in charge of a 'panama'.

Since there is a lock every three or four kilometres, and given that they are all connected by telephone, the location of any boat at any given time could be established and any vessel stopped.

Besides which, a police inspector from Épernay had

questioned everyone, and Maigret had been given transcripts of their written statements, which told him nothing except that the facts did not add up.

Everyone who had been in the Café de la Marine the previous day was known either to the owner of the bar or the lock-keeper and in most cases to both.

The carters spent at least one night each week in the same stable and invariably in the same, semi-drunken state.

'You know how it is! You take a drop at every lock . . . Nearly all the lock-keepers sell drink.'

The tanker-barge, which had arrived on Sunday afternoon and moved on again on Monday morning, was carrying petrol and was registered to a big company in Le Havre.

The *Providence*, which was owned by the skipper, passed this way twenty times a year with the same pair of horses and its old carter. And this was very much the case with all the others.

Maigret was in a tetchy mood. He entered the stable and from there went to the café or the shop any number of times.

He was seen walking as far as the stone bridge looking as though he was counting his steps or looking for something in the mud. Grimly, dripping with water, he watched as ten vessels were raised or lowered.

People wondered what he had in mind. The answer was: nothing. He didn't even try to find what might be called clues, but rather to absorb the atmosphere, to capture the essence of canal life, which was so different from the world he knew.

He had made sure that someone would lend him a bicycle if he should need to catch up with any of the boats.

The lock-keeper had let him have a copy of the *Official Handbook of Inland Waterways*, in which out-of-the-way places like Dizy take on an unsuspected importance for topographical reasons or for some particular feature: a junction, an intersection, or because there is a port or a crane or even an office.

He tried to follow in his mind's eye the progress of the barges and carters:

Ay – Port – Lock 13.

Mareuil-sur-Ay – Shipyard – Port – Turning dock – Lock 12 – Gradient 74, 36 . . .

Then Bisseuil, Tours-sur-Marne, Condé, Aigny . . .

Right at the far end of the canal, beyond the Langres plateau, which the boats reached by going up through a series of locks and then were lowered down the other side, lay the Sâone, Chalon, Mâcon, Lyons . . .

'What was the woman doing here?'

In a stable, wearing pearl earrings, her stylish bracelet and white buckskin shoes!

She must have been alive when she got there because the crime had been committed after ten in the evening.

But how? And why? And no one had heard a thing! She had not screamed. The two carters had not woken up.

If the whip had not been mislaid, it was likely the body might not have been discovered for a couple of weeks or a month, by chance when someone turned over the straw.

And other carters passing through would have snored the night away next to a woman's corpse!

Despite the cold rain, there was still a sense of something heavy, something forbidding in the atmosphere. And the rhythm of life here was slow.

Feet shod with boots or clogs shuffled over the stones of the lock or along the towpath. Tow-horses streaming with water waited while barges were held at the lock before setting off again, taking the strain, thrusting hard with their hind legs.

Soon evening would swoop down as it had the previous day. Already, barges travelling upstream had come to a stop and were tying up for the night, while their stiff-limbed crews made for the café in groups.

Maigret followed them in to take a look at the room which had been prepared for him. It was next door to the landlord's. He remained there for about ten minutes, changed his shoes and cleaned his pipe.

At the same time as he was going back downstairs, a yacht steered by a man in oilskins close to the bank slowed, went into reverse and slipped neatly into a slot between two bollards.

The man carried out all these manoeuvres himself. A little later, two men emerged from the cabin, looked wearily all round them and eventually made their way to the Café de la Marine.

They too had donned oilskins. But when they took them off, they were seen to be wearing open-necked flannel shirts and white trousers.

The watermen stared, but the newcomers gave no sign that they felt out of place. The very opposite. Their surroundings seemed to be all too familiar to them.

One was tall, fleshy, turning grey, with a brick-red face and prominent, greenish-blue eyes, which he ran over people and things as if he weren't seeing them at all.

He leaned back in his straw-bottomed chair, pulled another to him for his feet and summoned the landlord with a snap of his fingers.

His companion, who was probably twenty-five or so, spoke to him in English in a tone of snobbish indifference.

It was the younger man who asked, with no trace of an accent:

'You have still champagne? I mean without bubbles?'

'I have.'

'Bring us a bottle.'

They were both smoking imported cork-tipped Turkish cigarettes.

The watermen's talk, momentarily suspended, slowly started up again.

Not long after the landlord had brought the wine, the man who had handled the yacht arrived, also in white trousers and wearing a blue-striped sailor's jersey.

'Over here, Vladimir.'

The bigger man yawned, exuding pure, distilled boredom. He emptied his glass with a scowl, indicating that his thirst was only half satisfied.

'Another bottle!' he breathed at the young man.

The young man repeated the words more loudly, as if he was accustomed to passing on orders in this way.

'Another bottle! Of the same!'

Maigret emerged from his corner table, where he had been nursing a bottle of beer.

'Excuse me, gentlemen, would you mind if I asked you a question?'

The older man indicated his companion with a gesture which meant:

'Talk to him.'

He showed neither surprise nor interest. The sailor poured himself a drink and cut the end off a cigar.

'Did you get here along the Marne?'

'Yes, of course, along the Marne.'

'Did you tie up last night far from here?'

The big man turned his head and said in English:

'Tell him it's none of his business.'

Maigret pretended he had not understood and, without saying any more, produced a photograph of the corpse from his wallet and laid it on the brown oilcloth on the table.

The bargees, sitting at their tables or standing at the bar, followed the scene with their eyes.

The yacht's owner, hardly moving his head, looked at the photo. Then he stared at Maigret and murmured:

'Police?'

He spoke with a strong English accent in a voice that sounded hoarse.

'Police Judiciaire. There was a murder here last night. The victim has not yet been identified.'

'Where is she now?' the other man asked, getting up and pointing to the photo.

'In the morgue at Épernay. Do you know her?'

The Englishman's expression was impenetrable. But Maigret registered that his huge, apoplectic neck had turned reddish blue.

The man picked up his white yachting cap, jammed it on his balding head, then muttered something in English as he turned to his companion.

'More complications!'

Then, ignoring the gawping watermen, he took a strong pull on his cigarette and said:

'It's my wife!'

The words were less audible that the patter of the rain against the window panes or even the creaking of the windlass that opened the lock gates. The ensuing silence, which lasted a few seconds, was absolute, as if all life had been suspended.

'Pay the man, Willy.'

The Englishman threw his oilskin over his shoulders, without putting his arms in the sleeves, and growled in Maigret's direction.

'Come to the boat.'

The sailor he had called Vladimir polished off the bottle of champagne and then left, accompanied by Willy.

The first thing the inspector saw when he arrived on board was a woman in a dressing gown dozing on a dark-red velvet bunk. Her feet were bare and her hair uncombed.

The Englishman touched her on the shoulder and with the same poker face he had worn earlier he said in a voice entirely lacking in courtesy:

'Out!'

Then he waited, his eye straying to a folding table, where there was a bottle of whisky and half a dozen dirty glasses plus an ashtray overflowing with cigarette ends.

In the end, he poured himself a drink mechanically and

pushed the bottle in Maigret's direction with a gesture which meant:

'If you want one . . .'

A barge passed on a level with the portholes, and fifty metres further on the carter brought his horses to a halt. There was the sound of bells on their harness jangling.

2. The Passengers on Board the Southern Cross

Maigret was almost as tall and broad as the Englishman. At police headquarters on Quai des Orfèvres, his imperturbability was legendary. But now he was exasperated by the calm of the man he wanted to question.

Calm seemed to be the order of the day on the boat. From Vladimir, who sailed it, to the woman they had roused from her sleep, everyone on board seemed either detached or dazed. They were like people dragged out of bed after a night of serious drinking.

One detail among many: as she got up and looked round for a packet of cigarettes, the woman noticed the photo which the Englishman had put down on the table. During the short walk from the Café de la Marine to the yacht, it had got wet.

'Mary?' She put the question scarcely batting an eye.

'Yes. Mary.'

And that was it! She went out through a door which opened into the cabin and presumably was the door to the bathroom.

Willy appeared on deck and poked his head in through the hatchway. The cabin was cramped. Its varnished mahogany walls were thin and anyone forward could hear every word, for its owner looked first in that direction, frowning, then at the young man saying impatiently:

'Come in . . . and sharp about it!'

Then, turning to Maigret, he added curtly:

'Sir Walter Lampson, Colonel, Indian Army, retired.'

He accompanied this introduction of himself with a stiff little bow and a motion of the hand towards the bench seat along the cabin wall.

'And you are . . .?' said the inspector, turning towards Willy.

'A friend . . . Willy Marco.'

'Spanish?'

The colonel gave a shrug. Maigret scanned the young man's visibly Jewish features.

'My father is Greek and my mother Hungarian.'

'Sir Walter, I'm afraid I have to ask you some questions.'

Willy had sat down casually on the back of a chair and was rocking backwards and forwards, smoking a cigarette.

'I'm listening.'

But just as Maigret was about to open his mouth, the yacht's owner barked:

'Who did it? Do you know?'

He meant the perpetrator of the crime.

'We haven't come up with anything so far. That's why you can be useful to our inquiries by filling me in on a number of points.'

'Was it a rope?' he continued, holding one hand against his throat.

'No. The murderer used his hands. When was the last time you saw Mrs Lampson?'

'Willy . . . ?'

Willy was obviously his general factotum, expected to order the drinks and answer questions put to the colonel.

'Meaux. Thursday evening,' he said.

'And you did not report her disappearance to the police?'

Sir Walter helped himself to another whisky.

'Why should I? She was free to do whatever she pleased.'

'Did she often go off like that?'

'Sometimes.'

The sound of rain pattered on the deck overhead. Dusk was turning into night. Willy Marco turned the electric light on.

'Batteries been charged up?' the colonel asked him in English. 'It's not going to be like the other day?'

Maigret was trying to maintain a coherent line of questioning. But he was constantly being distracted by new impressions.

Despite his best efforts, he kept looking at everything, thinking about everything simultaneously. As a result his head was filled with a jumble of half-formed ideas.

He was not so much annoyed as made to feel uneasy by this man who, in the Café de la Marine, had cast a quick glance at the photo and said without flinching:

'It's my wife.'

And he recalled the woman in the dressing gown saying:

'Mary?'

Willy went on rocking to and fro, a cigarette glued to his lips, while the colonel was worrying about the boat's batteries!

In the neutral setting of his office, the inspector would have doubtless conducted a properly structured interview. But here, he began by taking off his overcoat without being invited to and picked up the photo, which was disturbing in the way all photographs of corpses are disturbing.

'Do you live here, in France?'

'In France, England . . . Sometimes Italy . . . Always on my boat, the *Southern Cross*.'

'And you've just come from . . . ?'

'Paris!' replied Willy who had got the nod from the colonel to do the talking. 'We stayed there two weeks after spending a month in London.'

'Did you live on board?'

'No. The boat was moored at Auteuil. We stayed at the Hotel Raspail, in Montparnasse.'

'You mean the colonel, his wife, the lady I saw just now, plus yourself?'

'Yes. The lady is the widow of a member of the Chilean parliament, Madame Negretti.'

Sir Walter gave an impatient snort and lapsed into English again:

'Get on with it or else he'll still be here tomorrow morning.'

Maigret did not flinch. But from then on, he put his questions with more than a touch of bloody-mindedness.

'So Madame Negretti is no relation?' he asked Willy.

'Absolutely not.'

'So she is not connected in any way with you and the colonel . . . Would you tell me about accommodation arrangements on board?'

Sir Walter swallowed a mouthful of whisky, coughed and lit a cigarette.

'Forward are the crew's quarters. That's where Vladimir sleeps. He's a former cadet in the Russian navy . . . He served in Wrangel's White Russian fleet.'

'Any other crew? No servants?'

'Vladimir does everything.'

'Go on.'

'Between the crew's quarters and this cabin are, on the right, the galley, and on the left the bathroom.'

'And aft?'

'The engine.'

'So there were four of you in this cabin?'

'There are four bunks . . . First, the two that you see. They convert to day couches . . . Then . . .'

Willy crossed to a wall panel, pulled out a kind of deep drawer which was in fact a bed.

'There's one of these on each side . . . Do you see?'

Actually, Maigret was indeed beginning to see a little more clearly. He was beginning to feel that it wouldn't be long before he got to the bottom of these unusual living arrangements.

The colonel's eyes were a dull grey and watered like a drunk's. He seemed to have lost interest in the conversation.

'What happened at Meaux? But first, when exactly did you get there?'

'Wednesday evening . . . Meaux is a one-day stage from

Paris. We'd brought along a couple of girls, just friends, with us from Montparnasse.'

'And?'

'The weather was marvellous. We played some records and danced outside, on deck. Around four in the morning I took the girls to their hotel, and they must have caught the train back the next morning.'

'Where was the *Southern Cross* moored?'

'Near the lock.'

'Anything happen on Thursday?'

'We got up very late, we were woken several times in the night by a crane loading stone into a barge nearby. The colonel and I went for a drink before lunch in town. Then, in the afternoon, let me see . . . the colonel had a nap . . . and I played chess with Gloria . . . Gloria is Madame Negretti.'

'On deck?'

'Yes. I think Mary went for a walk.'

'And she never came back?'

'Yes she did: she had dinner on board. The colonel suggested we all spend the evening at the palais de danse. Mary didn't want to come with us . . . When we got back, which was around three in the morning, she wasn't here.'

'Didn't you look for her?'

Sir Walter was drumming his fingers on the polished top of the table.

'As the colonel told you, his wife was free to come and go as she pleased. We waited for her until Saturday and then we moved on . . . She knew our route and could have caught up with us later.'

'Are you going down to the Mediterranean?'

'Yes, to the island of Porquerolles, off Hyères. It's where we spend most of the year. The colonel bought an old fort there. It's called the Petit Langoustier.'

'Did everybody stay on board all day Friday?'

Willy hesitated for a moment then almost blurted out his answer:

'I went to Paris.'

'Why?'

He laughed unpleasantly, which gave his mouth an odd twist.

'I mentioned our friends, the two girls . . . I wanted to see them again. Or at least one of them.'

'Can you give me their names?'

'First names . . . Suzy and Lia . . . You'll find them any night at La Coupole. They live at the hotel on the corner of Rue de la Grande-Chaumière.'

'Working girls?'

'They're both decent sorts . . .'

The door opened. It was Madame Negretti. She had put on a green silk dress.

'May I come in?'

The colonel answered with a shrug. He must now have been on to his third whisky and was drinking them more or less neat.

'Willy . . . Ask him . . . The formalities . . .'

Maigret had no need to have it translated to understand. But this roundabout, offhand way of being asked questions was beginning to irritate him.

'Obviously as a first step you will be expected to identify the body. After the post-mortem, you will no doubt be given a death certificate authorizing burial. You will choose the cemetery and . . .'

'Can we go now, straightaway? Is there a garage around here where I can hire a car?'

'There's one in Épernay.'

'Willy, phone for a car . . . right now.'

'There's a phone at the Café de la Marine,' said Maigret while the young man badtemperedly put on his oilskin jacket.

'Where's Vladimir?'

'I heard him come back a little while ago.'

'Tell him we'll have dinner at Épernay.'

Madame Negretti, who was running to fat and had glossy black hair and very light skin, had found a chair in a corner, under the barometer, and had observed what was happening with her chin cupped in one hand. She looked as if her mind was elsewhere or perhaps she was deep in thought.

'Are you coming with us?' asked Sir Walter.

'I'm not sure . . . Is it still raining?'

Maigret was already bristling, and the colonel's last question did nothing to calm him down.

'How many days do think you'll need us for? To wind everything up?'

To this came the blunt answer:

'Do you mean including the funeral?'

'Yes . . . Three days?'

'If the police doctors produce a burial certificate and if the examining magistrate has no objection, you could be all done in practical terms inside twenty-four hours.'

Did the colonel feel the bitter sarcasm of the words?

Maigret needed to take another look at the photo: a body that was broken, dirty, crumpled, a face which had once been pretty, carefully made up, with scented rouge applied to lips and cheeks, and a macabre grimace which you couldn't look at without feeling an icy chill run up and down your spine.

'Like a drink?'

'No thanks.'

'In that case . . .'

Sir Walter stood up to indicate that he considered that the interview was over. Then he called:

'Vladimir! . . . A suit!'

'I'll probably have to question you again,' the inspector said. 'I may even need to have your boat thoroughly searched.'

'Tomorrow . . . Épernay first, right? . . . How long will the car be?'

'Will I have to stay here by myself?' said Madame Negretti in alarm.

'With Vladimir . . . But you can come . . .'

'I'm not dressed.'

Willy suddenly burst in and shrugged off his streaming oilskins.

'The car will be here in ten minutes.'

'Perhaps, inspector, if you wouldn't mind . . . ?'

The colonel motioned to the door.

'We must dress.'

As he left, Maigret felt so frustrated that he would gladly have punched someone on the nose. He heard the hatch close behind him.

From the outside, all that could be seen was the glow of eight portholes and the light of the white lantern fixed to the mast. Not ten metres away was the outline of the squat stern of a barge and, on the left, a large heap of coal.

Perhaps it was an illusion but Maigret had the impression that the rain was coming down twice as hard and that the sky was the darkest and most threatening he'd ever seen.

He made his way to the Café de la Marine, where everyone stopped talking the moment he walked in. All the watermen were there, huddled round the cast-iron stove. The lock-keeper was leaning against the bar, near the landlord's daughter, a tall girl with red hair who wore clogs.

The tables were covered with waxy cloths and were littered with wine bottles, tumblers and standing pools of drink.

'So, was it his missus?' the landlord finally asked, taking his courage in both hands.

'Yes. Give me a beer. On second thoughts, no. Make it something hot. A grog.'

The watermen's talk started up again, very gradually. The girl brought Maigret the steaming glass and in doing so brushed against his shoulder with her apron.

The inspector imagined those three characters getting dressed in that cramped space. Vladimir too.

He imagined a number of other things, idly and without great relish.

He was familiar with the lock at Meaux, which is bigger than most locks because, like the one at Dizy, it is situated at the junction of the Marne and the canal, where there is a crescent-shaped port which is always full of barges packed closely together.

There, among the watermen, the *Southern Cross* would have been moored, all lit up, and on board the two women from Montparnasse, the curvaceous Gloria Negretti, Madame Lampson, Willy and the colonel dancing on the deck to the strains of the gramophone and drinking . . .

In a corner of the Café de la Marine, two men in blue overalls were eating sausage and bread, cutting slices off each with their knives and drinking red wine.

And someone was talking about an accident which had happened that morning in the 'culvert', that is a stretch of the canal which, as it crosses the high part of the Langres plateau, passes through a tunnel for eight kilometres.

A barge hand had got one foot caught in the horses' tow-line. He'd called out but hadn't been able to make the carter hear. So when the animals set off again after a rest stop, he'd been yanked into the water.

The tunnel was not lit. The barge carried only one lamp which reflected faintly in the water. The barge hand's brother – the boat was called *Les Deux Frères* – had jumped into the canal.

Only one of them had been fished out, and he was dead. They were still looking for the other.

'They only had two more instalments on the boat to pay. But it looks like, going by the contract, that the wives won't have to fork out another penny.'

A taxi-driver wearing a leather cap came in and looked round.

'Who was it ordered a car?'

'Me!' said Maigret.

'I had to leave it at the bridge. I didn't fancy finishing up in the canal.'

'Will you be eating here?' the landlord asked the inspector.

'I don't know yet.'

He went out with the taxi-driver. Through the rain, the white-painted *Southern Cross* was a milky stain. Two boys from a nearby barge, out despite the downpour, were staring at it admiringly.

'Joseph!' came a woman's voice. 'Bring your brother here! . . . You're going to get a walloping! . . .'

'*Southern Cross*,' the taxi-driver read on the bow. 'English, are they?'

Maigret walked across the gangplank and knocked. Willy opened the door. He was already dressed, looking elegant in a dark suit. Inside, Maigret saw the colonel, red-faced and jacketless, having his tie knotted by Gloria Negretti. The cabin smelled of eau de Cologne and brilliantine.

'Has the car come?' asked Willy. 'Is it here?'

'It's at the bridge, a short distance from here.'

Maigret stayed outside. He half heard the colonel and the young man arguing in English. Eventually Willy came out.

'He won't traipse through mud,' he said. 'Vladimir's going to launch the dinghy. We'll meet you there.'

'Thought so,' muttered the taxi-driver, who had heard.

Ten minutes later, Maigret and he were walking to and fro on the stone bridge just by the parked taxi, which had its sidelights on. Nearly half an hour went by before they heard the putt-putt of a small two-stroke engine.

Eventually Willy's voice shouted:

'Is this the place? . . . Inspector!'

'Yes, over here!'

The dinghy, powered by a removable motor, turned a half circle and pulled in to the bank. Vladimir helped the colonel out and made arrangements to pick them up when they got back.

In the car, Sir Walter did not speak. Despite his bulk, he was remarkably elegant. Ruddy-faced, well turned-out and impassive, he was every inch the English gentleman as portrayed in nineteenth-century prints.

Willy was chain-smoking.

'Some jalopy!' he muttered as they lurched over a drain.

Maigret noticed he was wearing a platinum ring set with a large yellow diamond.

When they got to the town, where the cobbled streets gleamed in the rain, the taxi-driver lifted the glass separating him and his fare and asked:

'Where do you want me to . . . ?'

'The mortuary!' replied the inspector.

It didn't take long. The colonel barely said a word. There was only one attendant in the building, where three bodies were laid out on stone slabs.

All the doors were locked. The locks creaked as they were opened. The light had to be switched on.

It was Maigret who lifted the sheet.

'Yes!'

Willy was the most upset, the most anxious to turn away from the sight.

'Do you recognize her too?'

'It's her all right . . . She looks so . . .'

He did not finish. The colour was visibly draining from his face. His lips were dry. If the inspector had not dragged him away, he would probably have passed out.

'You don't know who . . . ?' the colonel said distinctly.

Was a barely noticeable hint of distress just detectable in his tone of voice? Or wasn't it just the effect of all those glasses of whisky?

Even so, Maigret made a mental note of this small shift.

Then they were outside, on a pavement poorly lit by a single lamp-post near the car. The driver had not budged from his seat.

'You'll have dinner with us, won't you?' Sir Walter asked, again without turning to face Maigret.

'Thank you, no. Since I'm here, I'll make the most of it to sort out a few matters.'

The colonel bowed and did not insist.

'Come, Willy.'

Maigret remained for a moment in the doorway of the mortuary while the young man, after conferring with the Englishman, turned to the taxi-driver.

He was obviously asking which was the best restaurant in town. People walked past while brightly lit, rattling trams trundled by.

A few kilometres from there, the canal stretched away, and all along it, near the locks, there were barges now asleep which would set off at four in the morning, wrapped in the smell of hot coffee and stables.

3. Mary Lampson's Necklace

When Maigret got into bed, in his room, with its distinctive, slightly nauseating smell, he lay for some time aligning two distinct mental pictures.

First, Épernay: seen through the large, brightly lit windows of La Bécasse, the best restaurant in town, the colonel and Willy elegantly seated at a table surrounded by high-class waiters . . .

It was less than half an hour after their visit to the mortuary. Sir Walter Lampson was sitting ramrod straight, and the aloof expression on that ruddy face under its sparse thatch of silver hair was phenomenal.

Beside his elegance, or more accurately his pedigree, Willy's smartness, though he wore it casually enough, looked like a cheap imitation.

Maigret had eaten elsewhere. He had phoned the Préfecture and then the police at Meaux.

Then, alone and on foot, he had headed off into the rainy night along the long ribbon of road. He had seen the illuminated portholes of the *Southern Cross* opposite the Café de la Marine.

He had been curious and called in, using a forgotten pipe as an excuse.

It was there that he had acquired the second mental picture: in the mahogany cabin, Vladimir, still wearing his striped sailor's jersey, a cigarette hanging from his lips, was sitting opposite Madame Negretti, whose glossy hair again hung down over her cheeks.

They were playing cards – 'sixty-six', a game popular in central Europe.

There had been a brief moment of utter stupefaction. But no shocked reaction! Both had just stopped breathing for a second.

Then Vladimir had stood up and begun hunting for the pipe. Gloria Negretti had asked, in a faint lisp:

'Aren't they back yet? Was it Mary?'

The inspector had thought for a moment of getting on his bicycle, riding along the canal and catching up with the barges which had passed through Dizy on Sunday night. The sight of the sodden towpath and the black sky had made him change his mind.

When there was a knock on the door of his room, he was aware, even before he opened his eyes, that the bluey-grey light of dawn was percolating through the window of his room.

He had spent a restless night full of the sound of horses' hooves, confused voices, footsteps on the stairs, clinking glass in the bar underneath him and finally the smell of coffee and hot rum which had wafted up to him.

'What is it?'

'Lucas! Can I come in?'

Inspector Lucas, who almost always worked with Maigret, pushed the door open and shook the clammy hand which his chief held out through a gap in the bedclothes.

'Got something already? Not too worn out, I hope?'

'I'll survive, sir. After I got your phone call, I went straight to the hotel you talked about, on the corner of Rue de la Grande-Chaumière. The girls weren't there, but at least I got their names. Suzanne Verdier, goes under the name of Suzy, born at Honfleur in 1906. Lia Lauwenstein, born in the Grand Duchy of Luxembourg in 1903. The first arrived in Paris four years ago, started as a housemaid, then worked for a while as a model. The Lauwenstein girl has been living mainly on the Côte d'Azur . . . Neither, I checked, appears in the Vice Squad's register of prostitutes. But they might as well be on it.'

'Lucas, would you pass me my pipe and order me coffee?'

The sound of rushing water came from the chamber of the lock and over it the chug of a diesel engine idling. Maigret got out of bed and stood at a poor excuse for a washstand where he poured cold water into the bowl.

'Don't stop.'

'I went to La Coupole, like you said. They weren't there, but the waiters all knew them. They sent me to the Dingo, then La Cigogne. I ended up at a small American bar, I forget what it's called, in Rue Vavin, and found them there, all alone, looking very sorry for themselves. Lia is quite a looker. She's got style. Suzy is blonde, girl-next-door type, not a nasty bone in her body. If she'd stayed back in the sticks where she came from, she'd have got married and made a good wife and mother. She had got freckles all over her face and . . .'

'See a towel anywhere?' interrupted Maigret. His face was dripping with water, and his eyes were shut. 'By the way, is it still raining?'

'It wasn't raining when I got here, but it looks like it could start up again at any moment. At six this morning there was a fog which almost froze your lungs . . . Anyway, I offered to buy the girls a drink. They immediately asked for sandwiches, which didn't surprise me at first. But after a while I noticed the pearl necklace the Lauwenstein girl was wearing. As a joke I managed to get a bite on it. They were absolutely real! Not the necklace of an American millionairess, but even so it must have been worth all of 100,000 francs. Now when girls of that sort prefer sandwiches and hot chocolate to cocktails . . .'

Maigret, who was smoking his first pipe of the day, answered the knock of the girl who had brought his coffee. Then he glanced out of the window and registered that there was as yet no sign of life outside. A barge was passing close to the *Southern Cross*. The man leaning his back against the tiller was staring at the yacht with reluctant admiration.

'Right. Go on.'

'I drove them to another place, a quiet café.'

'There, without warning, I flashed my badge, pointed to the necklace and asked straight out: "Those are Mary Lampson's pearls, aren't they?"'

'I don't suppose they knew she was dead. But if they did, they played their parts to perfection.

'It took them a few moments to admit everything. In the end it was Suzy who said to her friend: "Best tell him the truth, seeing as he knows so much about it already."

'And a pretty tale it was too . . . Need a hand, chief?'

Maigret was flailing his arms wildly in his efforts to catch his braces, which were dangling down his thighs.

'The main point first. They both swore that it was Mary Lampson herself who gave them the pearls last Friday, in Paris, where she'd come to meet them. You'll probably understand this better than I do, because all I know about the case is what you told me over the phone.

'I asked if Madame Lampson had come there with Willy Marco. They said no. They said they hadn't seen Willy since last Thursday, when they left him at Meaux.'

'Just a moment,' Maigret broke in as he knotted his tie in a milky mirror which distorted his reflection. 'The *Southern Cross* arrives at Meaux on Wednesday evening. Our two girls are on board. They spend a lively night with the colonel, Willy, Mary Lampson and Gloria.

'It's very late when Suzy and Lia are taken off to a hotel, and they leave by train on Thursday morning . . . Did anyone give them money?'

'They said 500 francs.'

'Had they got to know the colonel in Paris?'

'A few days earlier.'

'And what happened on the yacht?'

Lucas gave a knowing smile.

'Assorted antics, none very savoury. Apparently the Englishman lives only for whisky and women. Madame Negretti is his mistress.'

'Did his wife know?'

'Oh, she knew all right! She herself was Willy's mistress. None of which stopped them bringing Suzy and Lia to join the party, if you follow me. And then there was Vladimir, who danced with all the women. In the early hours there was a row because Lia Lauwenstein said that 500 francs was charity. The colonel did not answer, leaving that to Willy. They were all drunk. The Negretti woman fell asleep on the roof, and Vladimir had to carry her into the cabin.'

Standing at the window, Maigret let his eye wander along the black line of the canal. To his left, he could see the small-gauge railway, which was still used to transport earth and gravel.

The sky was grey and streaked low down with shreds of blackish cloud. But it had stopped raining.

'What happened then?'

'That's more or less it. On Friday, Mary Lampson supposedly travelled to Paris and met up with both girls at La Coupole, when she must have given them the necklace.'

'My, my! A teeny-weeny little present . . .'

'Not a present. She handed it over for them to sell on. They were to give her half of whatever cash they got for it. She told them her husband didn't let her have much in the way of ready money.'

The paper on the walls of the room was patterned with small yellow flowers. On it the basin was a splash of dirty white.

Maigret saw the lock-keeper hurrying his way along with a bargee and his carter, clearly intending to drink a tot of rum at the bar.

'That's all I could get out of them,' said Lucas in conclusion. 'I left them at two this morning. I sent Inspector Dufour to keep a discreet eye on their movements. Then I went back to the Préfecture to check the records as per your instructions. I found the file on Willy Marco, who was kicked out of Monaco four years ago after some murky business to do with gambling. The following year he was questioned after an American woman claimed he had relieved her of some items of jewellery. But the charge was dropped, I don't know why, and Marco stayed out of jail. Do you think that he's . . .'

'I don't think anything. And that's the honest truth, I swear. Don't forget the murder was committed on Sunday after ten at night, when the *Southern Cross* was moored at La Ferté-sous-Jouarre.'

'What do you make of the colonel?'

Maigret shrugged his shoulders and pointed to Vladimir, who had just popped out through the forward hatch and was making for the Café de la Marine. He was wearing white trousers, rope sandals and a sweater. An American sailor's cap was pulled down over one ear.

'Phone call for Monsieur Maigret,' the red-haired serving girl called through the door.

'Come down with me, Lucas.'

The phone was in the corridor, next to a coat stand.

'Hello? . . . Meaux? . . . What was that? . . . Yes, the *Providence* . . . At Meaux all day Thursday loading? . . . Left at three o'clock Friday morning . . . Did any others? . . . The *Éco-III* . . . That's a tanker-barge, right? . . . Friday night at Meaux . . . Left Saturday morning . . . Thanks, inspector! . . . Yes, carry on with the questioning, you never know . . . Yes, I'll still be at this address . . .'

Lucas had listened to this conversation without understanding a word of it. Before Maigret could open his mouth to tell him, a uniformed officer on a bicycle appeared at the door.

'Message from Records . . . . It's urgent!'

The man was spattered with mud to the waist.

'Go and dry off for a moment and while you're at it drink my health with a hot grog.'

Maigret led Lucas out on to the towpath, opened the envelope and read out in a half-whisper:

> Summary of preliminary analyses relating to inquir-
> ies into the murder at Dizy:
> — victim's hair shows numerous traces of resin and
> also the presence of horsehairs, dark brown in
> colour;
> — the stains on the dress are fuel oil;
> — stomach contents at time of death: red wine and
> tinned meat similar in type to what is commercially
> available as corned beef.

'Eight out of ten horses have dark brown coats!' sighed Maigret.

In the café, Vladimir was asking what was the nearest place where he could buy the supplies he needed. There were three people who were telling him, including the cycling policeman from Épernay, who eventually set off with the Russian in the direction of the stone bridge.

Maigret, with Lucas in tow, headed for the stable, where, in addition to the landlord's grey, a broken-kneed mare possibly intended for slaughter had been kept since the night before.

'It wasn't here that she would have picked up traces of resin,' said the inspector.

He walked twice along the path that led round the buildings from the canal to the stable.

'Do you sell resin?' he asked when he saw the landlord pushing a wheelbarrow full of potatoes.

'It's not exactly proper resin . . . We call it Norwegian pitch. It's used for coating the sides of wooden barges above the waterline. Below it they use coal-tar, which is twenty times cheaper.'

'Have you got any?'

'There are still about twenty cans in the shop . . . But in this sort of weather there's no call for it. The bargees wait for the sun to come out before they start doing up their boats.'

'Is the *Éco-III* made of wood?'

'Iron, like most boats with motors.'

'How about the *Providence*?'

'Wood. Have you found out something?'

Maigret did not reply.

'You know what they're saying?' said the man, who had set down his wheelbarrow.

'Who are "they"?'

'Everybody on the canal, the bargees, pilots, lock-keepers. Goes without saying that a car would have a hard time driving along the towpath, but what about a motorbike? A motorbike could come from a long way off and leave no more trace than a pushbike.'

The door of the *Southern Cross*'s cabin opened. But no one came out.

For one brief moment, a patch of sky turned yellowish, as if the sun was at last about to break through. Maigret and Lucas walked up and down the canal bank without speaking.

No more than five minutes had gone by before the wind was bending the reeds flat, and one minute later rain was coming down in earnest.

Maigret held out one hand, an automatic reaction. With an equally mechanical gesture Lucas produced a packet of grey pipe tobacco from his pocket and handed it to his companion.

They paused a moment by the lock. The chamber was empty but it was being made ready, for an invisible tug still some distance off had hooted three times, which meant that it was towing three boats.

'Where do you reckon the *Providence* is now?' Maigret asked the lock-keeper.

'Half a mo' . . . Mareuil, Condé . . . and just before Aigny there's a string of about ten boats. That'll hold her up . . . Only two sluices of the lock at Vraux are working . . . So I'd say she's at Saint-Martin.'

'Is that far?'

'Exactly thirty-two kilometres.'

'And the *Éco-III*?'

'Should be at La Chaussée. But a barge coming downstream told us last night that she'd broken her propeller at Lock 12. Which means you'll find her at Tours-sur-Marne, which is fifteen kilometres upstream. It's their own fault . . . It's clear. Regulations state no loads should exceed 280 tons, but they all go on doing it.'

* * *

It was ten in the morning. As Maigret clambered on to the bicycle he had hired, he saw the colonel sitting in a rocking chair on the deck of the yacht. He was opening the Paris papers, which the postman had just delivered.

'No special orders,' he told Lucas. 'Stay around here. Don't let them out of your sight.'

The showers became less frequent. The towpath was dead straight. When he reached the third lock, the sun came out, still rather watery, but making the droplets of water on the reeds sparkle.

From time to time, Maigret had to get off his bike to get past horses towing a barge. Harnessed side by side, they took up the full width of the towpath and plodded forward, one step at a time, with an effort which made their muscles swell visibly.

Two of these animals were being driven by a little girl of eight or ten. She wore a red dress and carried a doll which dangled at the end of one arm.

The villages were, for the most part, some distance from the canal so that the long ribbon of flat water seemed to unfurl in an absolutely empty landscape.

Here and there was an occasional field with men bent over the dark earth. But most of it was woods. Reeds a metre and a half or two metres high further added to the mood of calm.

A barge taking on a cargo of chalk near a quarry sent up clouds of dust which whitened its hull and the toiling men.

There was a boat in the Saint-Martin lock, but it wasn't the *Providence*.

'They'll have stopped for their dinners in the reach above Châlons!' the lock-keeper's wife said as she went, with two young children clinging to her skirts, from one dock-gate to the other.

Maigret was not a man who gave up easily. Around eleven o'clock he was surprised to find himself in springlike surroundings, where the air pulsed with sun and warmth.

Ahead of him, the canal cut a straight line across a distance of six kilometres. It was bordered with woods of fir on both sides.

At the far end the eye could just make out the light-coloured stonework of a lock. Through its gates spurted thin jets of water.

Halfway along, a barge had halted, at a slight angle. Its two horses had been unharnessed and, their noses in a feedbag, were munching oats and snorting.

The first impression was cheerful or at least restful. Not a house in sight. The reflections in the calm water were wide and slow.

A few more turns of the pedals and the inspector saw a table set up under the awning over the tiller in the stern of the barge. On it was a blue and white checked waxed tablecloth. A woman with fair hair was setting a steaming dish in the middle of it.

He got off his bike after reading, on the rounded bows in gleaming polished letters: *Providence*.

One of the horses, taking its time, stared at him, then twitched its ears and let out a peculiar growl before starting to eat again.

* * *

Between the barge and the side of the canal was a thin, narrow plank, which sagged under Maigret's weight. Two men were eating, following him with their eyes, while the woman advanced towards him.

'Yes, what do you want?' she asked as she buttoned her blouse, which was part open over her ample bosom.

She spoke with a singsong intonation almost as strong as a southern accent. But she wasn't at all bothered. She waited. She seemed to be protecting the two men with the fullness of her brazen flesh.

'Information,' said the inspector. 'I expect you know there was a murder at Dizy?'

'The crew of the *Castor et Pollux* told us about it. They overtook us this morning. Is it true? It doesn't hardly seem possible, does it? How could anybody have done such a thing? And on the canal too, where it's always so peaceful.'

Her cheeks were blotchy. The two men went on eating, never taking their eyes off Maigret, who glanced involuntarily down at the dish which contained dark meat and gave off an aroma which startled his nostrils.

'A kid goat. I bought it this morning at the lock at Aigny . . . You were looking for information? About us, I suppose? We'd gone long before any dead body was discovered. Speaking of which, anybody know who the poor woman was?'

One of the men was short, dark-haired, with a drooping moustache and a soft, submissive air about him.

He was the husband. He'd merely nodded vaguely at the intruder, leaving his wife to do the talking.

The other man was around sixty years of age. His hair, thick and badly cut, was white. A beard three or four centimetres long covered his chin and most of his cheeks, and he had very thick eyebrows. He looked as hairy as an animal.

In contrast, his eyes were bright but without expression.

'It's your carter I'd like to talk to.'

The woman laughed.

'Talk to Jean? I warn you, he don't talk much to anyone. He's our tame bear! Look at the way he's eating! But he's also the best carter you could hope to find.'

The old man's fork stopped moving. He looked at Maigret with eyes that were disturbingly clear.

Village idiots sometimes have eyes like that. And also animals who are used to being treated with kindness and then without warning are beaten without pity.

There was something vacant about them. But something else too, something beyond words, almost withdrawn.

'What time did you get up to see to your horses?'

'Same time as always . . .'

Jean's shoulders were unusually broad and looked even broader because his legs were short.

'Jean gets up every day at half past two!' the woman broke in. 'Take a look at the horses. They are groomed every day like they're thoroughbreds. And of an evening, you won't get him to go near a drop of white wine until he's rubbed them down.'

'Do you sleep in the stable?'

Jean did not seem to understand. So it was again the woman who pointed to a structure, taller than the rest, in the middle of the boat.

'That's the stable,' she said. 'He always sleeps there. Our cabin is in the stern. Would you like to see it?'

The deck was spotlessly clean, the brasses more highly polished than those on the *Southern Cross*. And when the woman opened a double door made of pine with a sky-light of coloured glass over it, Maigret saw a touching sight.

Inside was a small parlour. It contained exactly the same oak Henri III-style furniture as is found in the most traditional of lower-middle-class front rooms. The table was covered with a cloth embroidered with silks of various colours, and on it were vases, framed photographs and a stand overflowing with green-leaved plants.

There was more embroidery on a dresser. Over the armchairs were draped thin dust covers.

'If Jean had wanted, we could have rigged up a bed for him near us . . . But he always says he can only sleep in the stable, though we're afraid that he'll get kicked one of these days. No good saying the horses know him, is it? When they're sleeping . . .'

She had started eating, like the housewife who makes other people's dinners and gives herself the worst portion without a second thought . . .

Jean had stood up and kept staring at his horses and then at the inspector while the skipper rolled a cigarette.

'And you didn't see anything, or hear anything?' asked Maigret, looking the carter directly in the eye.

The man turned to the skipper's wife, who replied with her mouth full:

'If he'd seen something, he'd have said, 'course he would.'

'Here's the *Marie*!' said her husband anxiously.

The chugging of an engine had become audible in the last few moments. Now the form of a barge could be made out astern of the *Providence*.

Jean looked at the woman, who was looking uncertainly at Maigret.

'Listen,' she said finally, 'if you've got to talk to Jean, would you mind doing it as we go? The *Marie* has got an engine, but she's slower than us. If she gets in front of us before we get to the lock, she'll hold us up for two days.'

Jean had not waited to hear her last words. He had already taken the feedbags containing the horses' oats from over their heads and was now driving them a hundred metres ahead of the barge.

The bargee picked up a tin trumpet and blew a few quavering notes.

'Are you staying on board? Listen, we'll tell you what we know. Everybody on the canals knows who we are, from Liège to Lyons.'

'I'll meet up with you at the lock,' said Maigret, whose bicycle was still on the bank.

The gangplank was stowed on board. A distant figure had just appeared on the lock gates, and the sluices started to open. The horses set off with a jangle of tinkling bells, and the red pompons tied to the top of their heads bobbed and jounced.

Jean walked by the side of them, unconcerned.

Two hundred metres astern, the motor barge slowed as it realized it had come too late.

Maigret followed, holding the handlebars of his bicycle with one hand. He could see the skipper's wife rushing to finish eating and her husband, short, thin and frail, leaning, almost lying, on the long tiller, which was too heavy for him.

4. The Lover

'I've had lunch,' said Maigret as he strode into the Café de la Marine, where Lucas was sitting at a table in the window.

'At Aigny?' asked the landlord. 'My brother-in-law's the inn-keeper at Aigny . . .'

'Bring us two beers.'

It had been a narrow escape. The inspector, pedalling hard, was barely in sight of Dizy when the weather had turned overcast again. And now thick rain was being drawn like curtains over the last rays of the sun.

The *Southern Cross* was still in its berth. There was no one to be seen on deck. And no sound came from the lock so that, for the first time, Maigret was aware of being truly in the country. He could hear chickens clucking in the yard outside.

'Got anything for me?' he asked Lucas.

'The Russian came back with supplies. The woman put in a brief appearance in a blue dressing gown. The colonel and Willy came for a drink before lunch. They gave me some odd looks, I think.'

Maigret took the tobacco pouch which his companion was holding out for him, filled his pipe and waited until the landlord, who had served them, had vanished into his shop.

'I didn't get anything either,' he muttered. 'Of the two boats which could have brought Mary Lampson here, one has broken down about fifteen kilometres from here, and the other is ploughing along the canal at three kilometres an hour.'

'The first one is iron-built, so no chance of the body coming into contact with pitch there.

'The other one is made of wood . . . The master and his wife are called Canelle. A fat motherly sort, who tried her level best to get me to drink a glass of disgusting rum, with a pint-sized husband who runs round after her like a spaniel.

'Which leaves just their carter.

'Either he's pretending to be stupid, in which case he does a brilliant turn, or else he's a complete half-wit. He's been with them for eight years. If the husband is a spaniel, he's a bulldog.

'He gets up at half past two every morning, sees to his horses, downs a bowl of coffee and then starts walking alongside his animals.

'He does his daily thirty or forty kilometres like that, every day, at the same pace, with a swig of white wine at every lock.

'Every evening he rubs the horses down, eats without speaking a word and then collapses on to a straw truss, most times still in his clothes.

'I've checked his papers. An old army pay book with pages so stuck together with filth they can hardly be opened. The name in it is Jean Liberge, born in Lille in 1869.

'And that's it . . . no, just a moment. The *Providence*

would have had to get Mary Lampson on board on Thursday evening at Meaux. So she was alive then. She was still alive when she got here on Sunday evening.

'It would be physically impossible to hide a grown woman for two days against her will in the stable on the boat.

'In which case all three of them would be guilty.'

The scowl on Maigret's face showed that he did not believe that was the case.

'But let's suppose the victim did get on the boat of her own free will. Do you know what you are going to do, Lucas? You're going to ask Sir Walter what his wife's maiden name was. Then get on the phone and find out what you can about her.'

There were two or three patches of sky where the sunlight still lingered, but the rain was coming down more and more heavily. Lucas had hardly left the Café de la Marine and was heading towards the yacht, when Willy Marco stepped off it, wearing a suit and tie, loose-limbed and casual, looking at nothing in particular.

It was definitely a trait shared by all the passengers on the *Southern Cross* that they always looked as though they hadn't had enough sleep or as if large amounts of alcohol did not agree with them.

The two men passed each other on the towpath. Willy appeared to hesitate when he saw Lucas go aboard. Then, lighting a fresh cigarette with the one he had just finished, he made straight for the café.

He was looking for Maigret and did not pretend otherwise.

He did not take off his soft felt hat but touched it absently with one finger as he murmured:

'Hello, inspector. Sleep well? I wanted a quick word . . .'

'I'm listening.'

'Not here, if it's all the same to you. Could we possibly go up to your room, do you think?'

He had lost nothing of his relaxed, confident manner. His small eyes sparkled with something not far from glee-ful elation, or perhaps it was malevolence.

'Cigarette?'

'No thanks.'

'Of course! You're a pipe man.'

Maigret decided to take him up to his room, though it hadn't yet been cleaned. After a glance out at the yacht, Willy sat down at once on the edge of the bed and began:

'Naturally you've already made inquiries about me.'

He looked round for an ashtray, failed to locate one and flicked his ash on to the floor.

'Not much to write home about, eh? But I've never claimed to be a saint. Anyway the colonel tells me what a rotter I am three times a day.'

What was remarkable about this was the completely frank expression on his face. Maigret was forced to admit that he was beginning to warm to Willy, who he hadn't been able to stomach at first.

A strange mixture. Sly and foxy. Yet at the same time a spark of decency which redeemed the rest, plus an engaging touch of humour.

'But you will have noted that I went to Eton, like the Prince of Wales. If we'd been the same age, we would have been the best of pals. But the truth is my father is a fig wholesaler in Smyrna. I can't bear the thought! I've been in some scrapes. The mother of one of my Eton friends, if you must know, got me out of one of them.

'You do understand if I don't give you her name, don't you? A delectable lady . . . But her husband became a government minister, and she was afraid of compromising his position.

'After that . . . They must have told you about Monaco, then that unpleasantness in Nice. Actually the truth isn't as bad as all that . . . Here's a tip: never believe anything you're told by a middle-aged American woman who lives it up on the Riviera and has a husband who arrives unexpectedly from Chicago. Stolen jewels have not always been stolen. But let's move on.

'Now, about the necklace. Either you know already or maybe you've not yet heard. I would have preferred to talk to you about it last night, but in the circumstances it might not have been the decent thing to do.

'The colonel is nothing if not a gentleman. He may be a touch over-fond of whisky, I grant. But he has some justification.

'He should have ended up a general. He was one of the men most in the public eye in Lima. But there was a scandal involving a woman, the wife of a highly placed local bigwig, and he was pensioned off.

'You've seen him. A magnificent specimen, with vigorous appetites. Out there, he had thirty native boys, orderlies, secretaries and God knows how many cars and horses for his own use.

'Then all of a sudden, all gone! Something like a hundred thousand francs a year, wiped out.

'Did I say that he'd already been married twice before he met Mary? His first wife died in India. Second time round, he got a divorce by taking all the fault on himself after finding his lady in bed with one of the boys.

'A real gentlemen!'

Willy, now leaning well back, was swinging one leg lethargically, while Maigret, his pipe between his teeth, stood with his back against the wall without moving.

'That's how it goes. Nowadays, he passes the time as well as he can. Down at Porquerolles, he lives in his old fort, which the locals call the Petit Langoustier. When he's saved up enough money, he goes to Paris or London.

'And just think that in India he used to give dinners for thirty or forty guests every week!'

'Was it about the colonel you wanted to talk to me?' murmured Maigret.

Willy did not bat an eyelid.

'Actually, I was trying to put you in the picture. I mean, you've never lived in India or London or had thirty native servants and God knows how many pretty girls at your beck and call . . . I'm not trying to get under your skin . . .

'Be that as it may, I met him two years ago.

'You didn't know Mary when she was alive . . . An adorable creature but a brain like a bird's . . . And a touch loud. If you weren't waiting hand and foot on her all the time, she'd have a fit or cause a scene.

'By the way, do you know how old the colonel is? Sixty-eight.

'She wore him out, if you follow me. She happily indulged his fantasies – he's not past it yet! – but she could be a bit of a nuisance.

'Then she got a thing about me. I quite liked her.'

'I take it that Madame Negretti is Sir Walter's mistress?'

'Yes,' the young man agreed with a scowl. 'It's hard to explain . . . He can't live or drink on his own. He has to have people round him. We met her when we put in once at Bandol. The next morning, she didn't leave. As far as he's concerned, that was it. She'll stay as long as she likes.

'But me, I'm different. I'm one of those rare men who can hold his whisky as well as the colonel.

'Except perhaps for Vladimir, who you've seen. Nine times out of ten, he's the one who puts us both to bed in our bunks.

'I don't know if you have grasped my position. It's true that I have no material worries. Still, there are times when we get stuck in a port for a fortnight waiting for a cheque from London so that we can buy petrol!

'Yes, and that necklace, which I shall come back to in a moment, has seen the inside of a pawnshop a score of times.

'Never mind! The whisky rarely runs out.

'It's not exactly a lavish lifestyle. But we sleep for as long as we want. We come and we go.

'Speaking personally, I much prefer it to being knee-deep in my father's figs.

'At the beginning, the colonel bought several items of jewellery for his wife. From time to time she would ask him for money.

'To buy clothes and so that she had a little pocket-money, if you follow me.

'But whatever you might think, I swear I got a colossal shock yesterday when I realized it was her in that awful photo! So did the colonel, actually . . . But he'd go through fire and water rather than show his feelings. That's his style. And so very English!

'When we left Paris last week – it's Tuesday today, isn't it – the cash was running low. The colonel sent a cable to London asking for an advance on his pension. We waited for it at Épernay. The draft arrived at around this time of day, I think.

'Thing is, I'd left a few debts unpaid in Paris. I'd asked Mary once or twice why she didn't sell her necklace. She could easily have told her husband she'd lost it or said it had been stolen.

'Thursday evening was the party, as you know. But you really shouldn't get any wrong ideas about what went on. The moment Lampson catches sight of pretty women, he has to invite them on board.

'Then a couple of hours later, when he's had too much to drink, he tells me to get rid of them as cheaply as possible.

'On Thursday, Mary got up much earlier than usual, and by the time we'd all staggered out of our bunks, she'd already gone outside.

'After lunch, there was a brief moment when the two of us were alone. She was very affectionate. Affectionate in a special way, a sad way.

'At one point, she put her necklace in my hand and said: "Just sell it."

'I'm sorry if you don't believe me . . . I felt awkward, had a qualm or two. If you'd known her, you'd understand.

'Although she could be a real bitch at times, at others she could be quite touching.

'Don't forget that she was over forty. She was looking out for herself. But she must have had an inkling that her time had gone.

'Then someone came in. I slipped the necklace into my pocket. In the evening, the colonel dragged us all off to the palais de danse, and Mary stayed on board by herself.

'When we got back, she wasn't there. Lampson wasn't worried. It wasn't the first time she'd run off like that.

'And not for the reasons you might think. On one occasion, for instance, during the festival of Porquerolles, there was a rather jolly orgy at the Petit Langoustier which lasted the best part of a week. For the first couple of days, Mary was the life and soul of the party. But on day three, she disappeared.

'And do you know where we found her? Staying at an inn at Giens, where she was happily passing the time playing mummies with a couple of unwashed brats.

'I was not comfortable with the business of the necklace. On Friday, I went up to Paris. I nearly sold it. But then I told myself that if there were problems I could land myself in serious trouble.

'Then I remembered the two girls from the night before. With girls like that, you can get away with anything. Besides, I'd already met Lia in Nice and knew I could count on her.

'I gave the necklace to her. Just in case, I told her that if anyone asked, she was to say that Mary herself had given it to her to sell.

'It's as simple as that, and very stupid! I would have been far better off keeping quiet. All the same, if I come up against policemen who aren't very bright, it's the sort of thing that could well land me in court.

'I realized this yesterday the minute I heard that Mary had been strangled.

'I won't ask you what you think. To be honest, I'm expecting to be arrested.

'That would be a mistake, a big mistake! Look, if you want me to help, I'm ready to lend you a hand.

'There are things that may strike you as odd but are quite straightforward really.'

He was now almost flat on the bed, still smoking, with his eyes fixed on the ceiling.

Maigret took up a position by the window to cover his perplexity.

'Does the colonel know that you're here telling me all this?' he asked, turning round suddenly.

'No more than he knows about the business with the necklace. Actually, though I'm obviously in no position to ask, I would prefer if he went on not knowing.'

'And Madame Negretti?'

'A dead weight. A beautiful woman who is incapable of existing except on a couch, smoking cigarettes and drinking sweet liqueurs. She started the day she first came on board and has been doing it ever since . . . Oh sorry: she also plays cards. I think it's the only thing that really interests her.'

The screech of rusted iron indicated that the lock gates were being opened. Two mules trudged past the front of the house then stopped a little further on, while an empty barge continued moving, swinging as it lost way, looking as though it were trying to climb up the bank.

Vladimir, bent double, was baling out the rainwater which threatened to swamp the dinghy.

A car crossed the stone bridge, attempted to drive on to the towpath, stopped, then made several clumsy attempts to turn before coming to a complete stop.

A man dressed all in black got out. Willy, who had got off the bed, glanced out of the window and said:

'It's the undertaker.'

'When is the colonel thinking of leaving?'

'Immediately after the funeral.'

'Which will take place here?'

'Anywhere'll do! He already has one wife buried near Lima and another now married to a New Yorker who will finish up under six feet of American soil.'

Maigret glanced across at him instinctively, as if he was trying to work out if he was joking. But Willy Marco was perfectly serious, though that little ambiguous spark still flickered in his eye.

'If, that is, the money draft has come through! Otherwise, the funeral will have to wait.'

The man in black halted uncertainly by the yacht, put a question to Vladimir, who answered without stopping what he was doing, then finally climbed aboard and vanished into the cabin.

Maigret had not seen Lucas come out.

'You'd better go,' he said to Willy.

Willy hesitated. For a moment, a look of anxiety flitted across his face.

'Are you going to ask him about the necklace?'

'I don't know.'

The moment had passed. Willy, his usual cool self once more, knocked out the dent in his felt hat, waved a good-bye with one hand and went downstairs.

When, shortly after, Maigret followed him down, there were two bargees leaning on the bar nursing bottles of beer.

'Your mate's on the phone,' said the landlord. 'Asked for a Moulins number.'

A tug sounded its hooter several times in the distance. Maigret counted mechanically and muttered:

'Five.'

On the canal it was business as usual. Five barges approaching. The lock-keeper, wearing clogs, emerged from his house and made for the sluices.

Lucas came out of the phone booth. His face was red.

'Whew! That was hard work . . .'

'What is it?'

'The colonel told me his wife's maiden name was Marie Dupin. For the wedding, she produced a birth certificate with that name on it issued at Moulins. Now I've just phoned them there, pulling rank . . .'

'And?'

'There's only one Marie Dupin on their register. She is forty-two years old, has three children and is married to a man called Piedbœuf, who is a baker in the high street.

The clerk in the town hall I talked to said she had seen her serving in the shop only yesterday. Apparently she weighs all of 180 pounds.'

Maigret said nothing. Looking like a well-to-do bystander with time on his hands, he wandered over to the lock without another thought for his companion and followed every stage of the operation closely. All the while, one thumb angrily tamped down the tobacco in his pipe.

A little later, Vladimir approached the lock-keeper. He touched his white forage cap with one hand and asked where he could fill up with fresh water.

5. The YCF Badge

Maigret had gone to bed early, while Inspector Lucas, who had his orders, went off to Meaux, Paris and Moulins.

When he left the bar, there had been three customers, two bargees and the wife of one of them who had joined her husband and was sitting in a corner, knitting.

The atmosphere was cheerless and heavy. Outside, a barge had tied up less than two metres from the *Southern Cross*, whose portholes were all lit up.

Now, suddenly, the inspector was dragged from a dream so confused that even as he opened his eyes he could remember nothing of it. Someone was knocking urgently on his door, and a voice was calling in a panic:

'Inspector! Inspector! Come quickly! My father . . .'

He ran to the door in his pyjamas and opened it. Outside he was surprised to see the landlord's daughter looking distraught. She leaped on him and literally buried herself in his arms.

'Ah! . . . You must go, hurry! . . . No, stay here! . . . Don't leave me by myself! . . . I couldn't bear it! . . . I'm scared! . . .'

He had never paid much attention to her. He'd thought she was a sturdy girl, well upholstered, but without a nerve in her body.

And here she was, face convulsed, heaving for breath,

hanging on to him with an insistence that was embarrassing. Still trying to extricate himself, he moved towards the window and opened it.

It was probably about six in the morning. It was barely first light and cold as a winter dawn.

A hundred metres beyond the *Southern Cross*, in the direction of the stone bridge and the Épernay road, four or five men were using a heavy boat hook to fish out something floating in the water, while one of the barge men untied his dinghy and began rowing across.

Maigret's pyjamas had seen better days. He threw his overcoat over his shoulders, located his ankle boots and inserted his bare feet into them.

'You realize . . . It's *him*! . . . They've . . .'

With a sudden movement, he broke free of the clutches of this strange girl, hurried down the stairs and was going outside just as a woman carrying a baby in her arms was bearing down on the group.

He hadn't been there when Mary Lampson's body had been found. But this new discovery was if anything more grim because, as an effect of this recurrence of crime, a feeling of almost mystical anguish now hung over this stretch of the canal.

The men called to each other. The landlord of the Café de la Marine, who had been first to spot a body floating in the water, was directing operations.

Twice the boat hook had snagged the corpse and each time the metal end had slipped. Each time, the body had dipped a few centimetres before returning to the surface.

Maigret had already recognized Willy's dark suit. He

61

could not see the face because the head, being heavier, remained submerged.

The man in the dinghy suddenly nudged it, grabbed the body by the chest and raised it with one hand. But he had to haul it over the side of the boat.

The man was not squeamish. He lifted the legs one after the other, threw his mooring rope on to the bank then wiped his streaming forehead with the back of his hand.

For one moment, Maigret had a glimpse of Vladimir's sleep-dulled head appearing through a hatch on the yacht. The Russian rubbed his eyes. Then he vanished.

'Don't touch anything!'

Behind him, one of the men protested, saying that back in Alsace his brother-in-law had been revived after being in the water for nearly three hours.

The landlord of the café pointed to the corpse's throat. There was no doubt: two finger marks, black, just like the ones on the neck of Mary Lampson.

This death was the more shocking of the two. Willy's eyes were wide open, looking much, much larger than usual. His right hand was still clutching a handful of reeds.

Maigret suddenly sensed an unexpected presence behind him. He turned and saw the colonel, also in pyjamas with a silk dressing gown thrown over them and blue kid slippers on his feet.

His silver hair was dishevelled and his face slightly puffy. He was a strange sight dressed like that, surrounded by canal men wearing clogs and thick coarse clothes, in the mud and damp of the early morning.

He was the tallest and broadest there. He gave off a faint whiff of eau de Cologne.

'It's Willy!' he said in a hoarse whisper.

Then he said a few words in English, too fast for Maigret to understand, bent down and touched the face of the young man.

The girl who had woken the inspector was leaning on the café door for support, sobbing. The lock-keeper came running.

'Phone the police at Épernay . . . And a doctor . . .'

Even Madame Negretti came out, barely decent, with nothing on her feet. But she did not dare leave the bridge of the yacht and called to the colonel:

'Walter! Walter!'

In the background were people who had arrived unseen: the driver of the little train, a group of navvies and a man with a cow which went ambling along the towpath by itself.

'Take him inside the café . . . And don't touch him more than you have to.'

He was obviously dead. The elegant suit, now no more than a limp rag, trailed along the ground when the body was lifted.

The colonel followed slowly. His dressing gown, blue slippers and ruddy scalp, across which the wind stirred a few long wisps of hair, made him an absurd but also priestly figure.

The girl's sobs came faster when the body passed in front of her. Then she ran off and shut herself away in the kitchen. The landlord was yelling down the phone:

'No, operator! . . . Police! . . . Hurry up! . . . There's been a murder! . . . Don't hang up! . . . Hello? Hello?'

Maigret kept most of the onlookers out. But the barge men who had discovered the body and helped to fish it out had all crowded into the café where the tables were still littered with glasses and bottles from the night before. The stove roared. A broom was lying in the middle of the floor.

The inspector caught a glimpse of Vladimir peering in through one of the windows. He'd had time to put his American sailor's forage cap on his head. The barge men were talking to him, but he was not responding.

The colonel was still staring at the body, which had been laid out on the red stone flags of the café floor. Whether he was upset or bored or scared it was impossible to say. Maigret went up to him:

'When was the last time you saw him?' he asked.

Sir Walter sighed and seemed to look around him for the man he usually relied on to answer for him.

'It's all so very terrible . . .' he said eventually.

'Didn't he sleep on board last night?'

With a gesture of the hand, the Englishman pointed to the barge men who were listening to them. It was like a reminder of the conventions. It meant: 'Do you think it right and proper for these people . . .'

Maigret ordered them out.

'It was ten o'clock last night. We had no whisky left on board. Vladimir hadn't been able to get any at Dizy. I decided to go to Épernay.'

'Did Willy go with you?'

'Not very far. He went off on his own just after the bridge.'

'Why?'

'We had words . . .'

And as the colonel said this, his eyes still drawn to the pinched, pallid, twisted features of the dead man, his own face crumpled.

Was it because he had not slept enough and that his flesh was puffy that he looked more upset? Perhaps. But Maigret would have sworn that there were tears lurking under those heavy eyelids.

'Did you have a bust-up?'

The colonel gave a shrug, as if resigning himself to hearing such a vulgar, ugly expression.

'Were you angry with him about something?'

'No! I wanted to know . . . I kept saying: "Willy, you're a rotter . . . But you've got to tell me . . ."'

He stopped, overcome. He looked around him so that he would not be mesmerized by the dead man.

'Did you accuse him of murdering your wife?'

He shrugged and sighed:

'He went off by himself. It's happened before, now and again. Next morning we'd drink the first whisky of the day together and put it out of our minds . . .'

'Did you walk all the way to Épernay?'

'Yes.'

'Did you drink a lot?'

The lingering look which the colonel turned on the inspector was abject.

'I also tried my luck at the tables, at the club . . . They'd

65

told me at La Bécasse that there was a gambling club . . .
I came back in a cab.'

'At what time?'

With a motion of the hand he intimated that he had no
idea.

'Willy wasn't in his bunk?'

'No. Vladimir told me as he was helping me undress
for bed.'

A motorcycle and sidecar pulled up outside the door. A
police sergeant dismounted, and the passenger, a doctor,
climbed out. The café door opened and then closed.

'Police Judiciaire,' said Maigret, introducing himself to his colleague from Épernay. 'Could you get these
people to keep back and then phone the prosecutor's
office . . .?'

The doctor needed only a brief look at the body before
saying:

'He was dead before he hit the water. Take a look at
these marks.'

Maigret had already seen them. He knew. He glanced
mechanically at the colonel's right hand. It was muscular,
with the nails cut square and prominent veins.

It would take at least an hour to get the public prosecutor
and his people together and ferry them to the crime
scene. Policemen on cycles arrived and formed a cordon
around the Café de la Marine and the *Southern Cross*.

'May I get dressed?' the colonel asked.

Despite his dressing gown, slippers and bare ankles, he
made a surprisingly dignified figure as he passed through

the crowd of bystanders. He had no sooner gone into the cabin than he poked his head out again and shouted:

'Vladimir!'

Then all the hatches on the yacht were shut.

Maigret was interviewing the lock-keeper, who had been called out to man his gates by a motorboat.

'I imagine that there is no current in a canal? So a body will stay in the place where it was thrown in?'

'In long stretches of the canal, ten or fifteen kilometres, that would be true. But this particular stretch doesn't go even five. If a boat passes through Lock 13, which is the one above mine, I smell water that's released arrive here a few minutes later. And if I put a boat going downstream through my lock, I take a lot of water out of the canal, and that creates a short-lived current.'

'What time do you start work?'

'Officially at dawn but actually a lot earlier. The horse-drawn boats, which move pretty slowly, set off at about three in the morning. More often than not, they put themselves through the lock without me hearing a thing . . . Nobody says anything because we know them all . . .'

'So this morning . . . ?'

'The Frédéric, which spent the night here, must have left around half past three and went through the lock at Ay at five.'

Maigret turned and retraced his steps. Outside the Café de la Marine and along the towpath, a few groups of men had gathered. As the inspector passed them on his way to the stone bridge, an old pilot with a grog-blossom nose came up to him:

'Want me to show you the spot where that young feller was thrown into the water?'

And looking very proud of himself, he glanced round at his comrades, who hesitated a moment before falling into step behind him.

The man was right. Fifty metres from the stone bridge, the reeds had been trampled over an area of several metres. They hadn't simply been walked on. A heavy object had been dragged across the ground. The tracks were wide where the reeds had been flattened.

'See that? I live half a kilometre from here, in one of the first houses you come to in Dizy. When I was coming in this morning, to check if there were any boats going down the Marne that needed me, it struck me as unusual. And then I found this on the towpath just by it.'

The man was tiresome, for he kept pulling funny faces and looking back at his companions, who were following at a distance.

But the object he produced from his pocket was of the greatest interest. It was a finely worked enamel badge. On it was a kedge anchor and the initials 'YCF'.

'Yachting Club de France,' said the pilot. 'They all wear them in their lapels.'

Maigret turned to look at the yacht, which was clearly visible some two kilometres away. Under the words *Southern Cross* he could just make out the same initials: YCF.

Paying no further attention to the man who had given him the badge, he walked slowly to the bridge. On his right, the Épernay road stretched away in a straight line, still glistening with last night's rain. Traffic drove along it at high speeds.

To the left, the road formed a bend as it entered the village of Dizy. On the canal beyond, several barges were lying up, undergoing repairs, just by the yards owned by the Compagnie Générale de Navigation.

Maigret walked back the way he'd come, feeling the tension mounting. The public prosecutor's officials would be arriving soon, and for an hour or two there would be the usual chaos, questions, comings and goings and a spate of wild theories.

When he was level with the yacht, everything was still all closed up. A uniformed officer was pacing up and down a little distance away, telling bystanders to move along, but failing to prevent two journalists from Épernay taking pictures.

The weather was neither fine nor foul. A luminous grey morning sky, unbroken, like a frosted glass ceiling.

Maigret walked across the gangplank and knocked on the door.

'Who is it?' came the colonel's voice.

He went in. He was in no mood to argue. He saw the Negretti woman, wearing no more clothes than before, hair hanging down over her face and neck, wiping away her tears and snivelling.

Sir Walter was sitting on the bench seat, holding out his feet to Vladimir, who was helping him on with a pair of chestnut-brown shoes.

Water had to be boiling somewhere on a stove because there was the hiss of escaping steam.

The two bunks slept in by the colonel and Gloria were still unmade. Playing cards were scattered on the table beside a map of France's navigable waterways.

And still there was that elusive, spicy smell which evoked bar, boudoir and secret amours. A white canvas yachting cap hung from the hat stand next to a riding crop with an ivory handle.

'Was Willy a member of the Yacht Club de France?' asked Maigret in as neutral a tone as he could manage.

The way the colonel shrugged his shoulders told him his question was absurd. And so it was. The YCF is one of the most exclusive clubs.

'But I am,' Sir Walter said casually. 'And of the Royal Yacht Club in England.'

'Would you mind showing me the jacket you were wearing last night?'

'Vladimir . . .'

He now had his shoes on. He stood up, bent down and opened a small cupboard, which had been turned into a liquor cabinet. There was no whisky in sight. But there were other bottles of spirits, over which he hesitated.

Finally he brought out a bottle of liqueur brandy and murmured offhandedly:

'What will you have?'

'Not for me, thanks.'

He filled a silver goblet which he took from a rack above the table, looked for the siphon, and frowned darkly like a man all of whose habits have been turned upside down and who feels hard done by.

Vladimir emerged from the bathroom with a black

tweed suit. A nod from his master instructed him to hand it to Maigret.

'The YCF badge was usually pinned to the lapel of this jacket?'

'Yes. How long are they going to be over there? Is Willy still on the floor of that café?'

He had emptied his glass while still standing, a sip at a time, and hesitated about whether he'd pour himself another.

He glanced out of the porthole, saw legs and grunted indistinctly.

'Will you listen to me for a moment, colonel?'

The colonel indicated that he was listening. Maigret took the enamel badge from his pocket.

'This was found this morning at the spot where Willy's body was dragged through a bank of reeds and dumped in the canal.'

Madame Negretti uttered a cry, threw herself on the plum-coloured plush of the bench seat and there, holding her head in her hands, she began to sob convulsively.

Vladimir, however, did not move. He waited for the jacket to be returned to him so that he could hang it back up in its place.

The colonel gave an odd sort of laugh and repeated four or five times:

'Yes! Yes!'

As he did so, he poured himself another drink.

'Where I come from, the police ask questions differently. They have to say that everything you say may be used as evidence against you. I'll say it once . . .

Shouldn't you be writing this down? I won't say it again . . .

'I was with Willy. We had words. I asked . . . It doesn't matter what I asked.

'He wasn't a rotter like the rest of them. Some rotters are decent fellows.

'I spoke too harshly. He grabbed my jacket just here . . .'

He indicated the lapels and looked out irritably at the feet encased in clogs or heavy shoes which were still visible through the portholes.

'That's all. I don't know, maybe the badge fell off then . . . It happened on the other side of the bridge.'

'Yet the badge was found on this side.'

Vladimir hardly seemed to be listening. He gathered up things that were lying about, went forward and returned unhurriedly.

In a very strong Russian accent, he asked Gloria, who wasn't crying any more but was lying flat on her back without moving, clutching her head with both hands:

'You want anything?'

Steps were heard on the gangplank. There was a knock on the door, and the sergeant said:

'Are you in there, inspector? It's the prosecutor's office . . .'

'I'm coming!'

The sergeant did not move, an unseen presence behind the mahogany door with brass handles.

'One more thing, colonel. When is the funeral?'

'Three o'clock.'

'Today?'

'Yes! I have no reason to stay on here.'

When he had drunk his third glass of three-star cognac, his eyes looked more clouded. Maigret had seen those eyes before.

Then, just as the inspector was about to leave, he asked, cool, casual, every inch the master of all he surveyed:

'Am I under arrest?'

At once, Madame Negretti looked up. She was deathly pale.

6. The American Sailor's Cap

The conclusion of the interview between the magistrate and the colonel was almost a solemn moment. Maigret, who stood slightly apart, was not the only one to notice it.

He caught the eye of the deputy public prosecutor and saw that he too had picked up on it.

The public prosecutor's team had gathered in the bar room of the Café de la Marine. One door led to the kitchen, from which came the clatter of saucepans. The other door, glass-panelled, was covered with stuck-on transparent adverts for pasta and rock soap through which the sacks and boxes in the shop could be seen.

The peaked cap of a policeman in uniform marched to and fro outside the window. Onlookers, silent but determined, had grouped a little further away.

A half-litre glass, with a small amount of liquid in it, was still standing beside a pool of wine on one of the tables.

The clerk of the court, seated on a backless bench, was writing. There was a peevish look on his face.

Once the statements had all been taken, the body had been placed as far from the stove as possible and temporarily covered with one of the brown oilcloths taken from a tabletop, leaving its disjointed boards exposed.

The smell had not gone away: spices, stables, tar and wine lees.

The magistrate, who was reckoned to be one of the most unpleasant in Épernay – he was a Clairfontaine de Lagny and proud of the aristocratic 'de' in the name – stood with his back to the fire and wiped his pince-nez.

At the start of the proceedings, he had said in English: 'I imagine you'd prefer us to use your language?'

He himself spoke it quite well with, perhaps, a hint of affectation, a slight screw of the lips standard among those who try – and fail – to reproduce the correct accent.

Sir Walter had accepted the offer. He had responded to every question slowly, his face turned to the clerk, who was writing, pausing from time to time to allow him to catch up.

He had repeated, without adding anything new, what he had told Maigret during their two interviews.

For the occasion, he had chosen a dark-blue double-breasted suit of almost military cut. To one lapel was pinned a single medal: the Order of Merit.

In one hand he held a peaked cap. On it was a broad gilt crest bearing the insignia of the Yachting Club de France.

It was very simple. One man asked questions and the other man invariably gave a slight, deferential nod before answering.

Even so, Maigret looked on admiringly but could not help feeling mortified as he remembered his own intrusive probings on board the *Southern Cross*.

His English was not good enough for him to grasp all the finer points. But he at least understood the broad meaning of the concluding exchanges.

'Sir Walter,' said the magistrate, 'I must ask you to

remain available until we have got to the bottom of both these appalling crimes. I am afraid, moreover, that I have no choice but to withhold permission for the burial of Lady Lampson.'

Another slight bow of the head.

'Do I have your authorization to leave Dizy in my boat?'

With one hand the colonel gestured towards the onlookers who had gathered outside, the scenery, even the sky.

'My home is on Porquerolles . . . it will take me a week just to reach the Saône.'

This time it was the turn of the magistrate to offer a respectful nod.

They did not shake hands, though they almost did. The colonel looked around him, appeared not to see either the doctor, who seemed bored, or Maigret, who avoided his eye, but he did acknowledge the deputy prosecutor.

The next moment he was walking the short distance between the Café de la Marine and the *Southern Cross*.

He made no attempt to go inside the cabin. Vladimir was on the bridge. He gave him his orders and took the wheel.

Then, to the amazement of the canal men and the bargees, they saw the Russian in the striped jersey disappear into the engine room, start the motor and then, from the deck, with a neat flick of the wrist, yank the mooring ropes free of the bollards.

Within moments, a small, gesticulating group began moving off towards the main road, where their cars were waiting. It was the public prosecutor's team.

Maigret was left standing on the canal bank. He had finally managed to fill his pipe and now thrust both hands into his pockets with a gesture that was distinctly proletarian, even more proletarian than usual, and muttered:

'Well, that's that!'

It was back to square one!

The investigation of the prosecutor's office had come up with only a few points. It was too early to tell if they were significant.

First: the body of Willy Marco, in addition to the marks of strangulation, also had bruises to the wrists and torso. The police surgeon ruled out an ambush but thought that a struggle with an exceptionally strong attacker was more likely.

Second: Sir Walter had stated that he had met his wife in Nice, where, although she had divorced her Italian husband, she was still using her married name of Ceccaldi.

The colonel's account had not been clear. His wilfully ambiguous statement let it be supposed that Marie Dupin, or Ceccaldi, was at that time virtually destitute and living on the generosity of a few friends, though without ever actually selling her body.

He had married her during a trip to London, and it was then that she had obtained from France a copy of her birth certificate in the name of Marie Dupin.

'She was a most enchanting woman.'

In his mind's eye Maigret saw the colonel's fleshy, dignified, ruddy face as he said these words, without affectation and with a sober simplicity which had seemed to impress the magistrate favourably.

He stepped back to allow the stretcher carrying Willy's body to pass.

Suddenly he shrugged his shoulders and went into the café, sat down heavily on a bench and called:

'Bring me a beer!'

It was the girl who served him. Her eyes were still red, and her nose shone. He looked up at her with interest and, before he could question her, she looked this way and that to make sure no one was listening, then murmured:

'Did he suffer much?'

She had a lumpish, unintelligent face, thick ankles and red beefy arms. Yet she was the only one who had given a second thought to the suave Willy, who perhaps had squeezed her waist as a joke the evening before – if, indeed, he had.

Maigret was reminded of the conversation he had had with the young man when he had been half stretched out on the unmade bed in his room, chain-smoking.

The girl was wanted elsewhere. One of the watermen called to her:

'Seems like you're all upset, Emma!'

She tried to smile and gave Maigret a conspiratorial look.

The canal traffic had been held up all morning. There were now seven vessels, three with engines, tied up outside the Café de la Marine. The bargees' wives came to the shop, and each one made the door bell jangle.

'When you're ready for lunch . . .' the landlord said to Maigret.

'In a while.'

And from the doorway, he looked at the spot where the *Southern Cross* had been moored only that morning.

The previous evening, two men, two healthy men, had stepped off it. They had walked off towards the stone bridge. If the colonel was to be believed, they'd separated after an argument, and Sir Walter had gone on his way along the three kilometres of empty, dead-straight road which led to the first houses of Épernay.

No one had ever seen Willy alive again. When the colonel had returned in a cab, he had not noticed anything unusual.

No witnesses! No one had heard anything! The butcher at Dizy, who lived 600 metres from the bridge, said his dog had barked, but he hadn't investigated and could not say what time it had been.

The towpath, awash with puddles and pools, had been used by too many men and horses for there to be any hope of finding any useful tracks.

The previous Thursday, Mary Lampson, also fit and well to all appearances, had left the *Southern Cross*, where she had been alone.

Earlier – according to Willy – she had given him a pearl necklace, the only valuable item of jewellery she owned.

After this there was no trace of her. She had not been seen alive again. Two days had gone by when no one had reported seeing her.

On Sunday evening, she lay strangled under a pile of straw in a stable at Dizy, a hundred kilometres from her point of departure, with two carters snoring just feet from her corpse.

That was all! The Épernay magistrate had ordered both bodies to be transferred to cold storage in the Forensic Institute.

The *Southern Cross* had just left, heading south, for Porquerolles, for the Petit Langoustier, which was no stranger to orgies.

Maigret, head down, walked all round the building of the Café de la Marine. He beat off a bad-tempered goose which bore down on him, its beak open and shrieking with rage.

There was no lock on the stable door, only a simple wooden latch. The hunting dog with an overfed paunch, which prowled round the yard, turned joyful circles and greeted him deliriously, as it did all visitors.

When he opened the door, the inspector was confronted by the landlord's grey horse, which was no more tethered now than on the other days, and made the most of the opportunity to go for a walk outside.

The broken-winded mare was still lying in its box, looking miserable.

Maigret moved the straw with his foot, as though hoping to find something he had missed on his first examination of the place.

Two or three times he repeated to himself crossly:

'Back to square one!'

He had more or less made up his mind to return to Meaux, even Paris, and retrace step by step the route followed by the *Southern Cross*.

There were all kinds of odds and ends lying around: old halters, bits of harness, the end of a candle, a broken pipe . . .

From a distance he noticed something white poking out of a pile of hay. He went over not expecting anything much. The next moment he was holding an American sailor's forage cap just like the one worn by Vladimir.

The material was spattered with mud and horse droppings and misshapen as though it had been stretched in all directions.

Maigret searched all around but failed to come up with anything else.

Fresh straw had been put down over the spot where the body had been found to make it seem less sinister.

'Am I under arrest?'

As he walked towards the stable door, he could not have said why the colonel's question should suddenly surface in his memory. He also saw Sir Walter, as boorish as he was aristocratic, his eyes permanently watering, the drunkenness always just beneath the surface and his amazing composure.

He thought back to the brief talk he had had with the supercilious magistrate in the bar of the café, with its tables covered in brown oilcloth, which, through a sprinkling of polite voices and refined manners, had been magically transformed for a short time into a sophisticated drawing room.

He kept turning the cap round and round in his hands, suspicious, with a calculating look in his eye.

'Tread carefully,' Monsieur de Clairfontaine de Lagny had told him as he took Maigret's hand lightly.

The goose, still furious, followed the horse, screeching abuse at it.

The horse, letting its large head hang down, snuffled among the rubbish littering the yard.

On each side of the door was an old milestone. The inspector sat down on one of them, still holding the cap and his pipe, which had gone out.

Directly ahead of him was a large dung heap, then a hedge with occasional gaps in it, and beyond were fields in which nothing was yet growing and hills streaked with black and white on which a cloud with a dark centre seemed to have rested its full weight.

From behind one edge of it sprang an oblique shaft of sunlight which created sparkles of light on the dung heap.

'*An enchanting woman,*' the colonel had said of Mary Lampson.

'*Nothing if not a gentleman!*' Willy had said of the colonel.

Only Vladimir had said nothing. He had just kept busy, buying supplies, petrol, filling up the tanks of drinking water, baling out the dinghy and helping his employer to dress.

A group of Flemings passed along the road, talking in loud voices. Suddenly, Maigret bent down. The yard was paved with irregular flagstones. Two metres in front of him, in the crack between two of them, something had just been caught by the sun and glinted.

It was a cufflink, gold with a platinum hatching. Maigret had seen a pair just like it the day before, on Willy's wrists, when he was lying on his bed blowing cigarette smoke at the ceiling and talking so unconcernedly.

He took no more interest in the horse or the goose or

any of his surroundings. Moments later, he was turning the handle that cranked the phone.

'Épernay . . . Yes, the mortuary! . . . This is the police!'

One of the Flemings was just coming out of the café. He stopped and stared at the inspector, who was extraordinarily agitated.

'Hello? . . . Inspector Maigret here, Police Judiciaire . . . You've just had a body brought in . . . No, not the car accident, this is about the man drowned at Dizy . . . That's right . . . Find the custody officer . . . Go through his effects, you'll find a cufflink . . . I want you to describe it to me . . . Yes, I'll hang on.'

Three minutes later, he replaced the receiver. He had the information. He was still holding the forage cap and the cufflink.

'Your lunch is ready.'

He didn't bother to answer the girl with red hair, though she had spoken as politely as she could. He went out feeling that perhaps he was now holding one end of the thread but also fearing he would drop it.

'The cap in the stables . . . The cufflink in the yard . . . And the YCF badge near the stone bridge . . .'

It was that way he now started walking, very fast. Ideas formed and faded in turns in his mind.

He had not gone a kilometre when he was astonished by what he saw dead ahead.

The *Southern Cross*, which had set off in a great haste a good hour before, was now moored on the right-hand side of the bridge, among the reeds. He couldn't see anyone on board.

But when the inspector was less than a hundred metres short of it, a car coming from the direction of Épernay pulled up on the opposite bank. It stopped near the yacht. Vladimir, still wearing sailor's clothes, was sitting next to the driver. He got out and ran to the boat. Before he reached it, the hatch opened, and the colonel came out on deck, holding his hand out to someone inside.

Maigret made no attempt to hide. He couldn't tell whether the colonel had seen him or not.

Then things happened fast. The inspector could not hear what was said, but the way the people were behaving gave him a clear enough idea of what was happening.

It was Madame Negretti who was being handed out of the cabin by Sir Walter. Maigret noted that this was the first time he had seen her wearing town clothes. Even from a distance it was obvious that she was very angry.

Vladimir picked up the two suitcases which stood ready and carried them to the car.

The colonel held out one hand to help her negotiate the gangplank, but she refused it and stepped forward so suddenly that she almost fell head first into the reeds.

She walked on without waiting for him. He followed several paces behind, showing no reaction. She jumped into the car still in the same furious temper, thrust her head angrily out of the window and shouted something which must have been either an insult or a threat.

However, just as the car was setting off, Sir Walter bowed courteously, watched her drive off and then went back to his boat with Vladimir.

Maigret had not moved. He had a very strong feeling

that a change had come over the Englishman.

He did not smile. He remained his usual imperturbable self. But, for example, just as he reached the wheelhouse in the middle of saying something, he put one friendly, even affectionate, hand on Vladimir's shoulder.

Their cast-off was brilliantly executed. There were just the two men on board now. The Russian pulled in the gangplank and with one smooth action yanked the mooring ring free.

The prow of the *Southern Cross* was fast in the reeds. A barge coming up astern hooted.

Lampson turned round. There was no way now he could not have seen Maigret but he gave no sign of it. With one hand, he let in the clutch. With the other, he gave the brass wheel two full turns, and the yacht reversed just far enough to free herself, avoided the bow of the barge, stopped just in time and then moved forward, leaving a wake of churning foam.

It had not gone a hundred metres when it sounded its hooter three times to let the lock at Ay know that its arrival was imminent.

'Don't waste time . . . Just drive . . . Catch up with that car if you can.'

Maigret had flagged down a baker's van, which was heading in the direction of Épernay. About a kilometre ahead they could see the car carrying Madame Negretti. It was moving slowly: the road was wet and greasy.

When the inspector had stated his rank, the van driver had looked at him with amused curiosity.

'Hop in. It won't take me five minutes to catch them up.'

'No, not too fast.'

Then it was Maigret's turn to smile when he saw that his driver was crouching over the steering wheel just like American cops do in car chases in Hollywood crime films.

There was no need to risk life and limb, nor any kind of complication. The car stopped briefly in the first street it came to, probably to allow the passenger to confer with the driver. Then it drove off again and halted three minutes later outside what clearly was a rather expensive hotel.

Maigret got out of the van a hundred metres behind it, thanked the baker, who refused a tip and, having decided he wanted to see more, parked a little nearer the hotel.

A porter carried both bags in. Gloria Negretti walked briskly across the pavement.

Ten minutes later, Maigret was talking to the manager.

'The lady who has just checked in?'

'Room 9. I thought there was something not quite right about her. I never saw anybody more on edge. She talked fast and used lots of foreign words. As far as I could tell, she didn't want to be disturbed and asked for cigarettes and a bottle of kümmel to be taken up to her room. I hope at least there's not going to be any scandal . . . ?'

'None at all!' said Maigret. 'Just some questions I need to ask her.'

He could not help smiling as he neared the door with the number 9 on it, for there was lots of noise coming from inside. The young woman's high heels clacked on the wooden floor in a haphazard way.

She was walking to and fro, up and down, in all directions. She could be heard closing a window, tipping out a suitcase, running a tap, throwing herself on to the bed, getting up and kicking off a shoe to the other end of the room.

Maigret knocked.

'Come in!'

Her voice was shaking with anger and impatience. Madame Negretti had not been there ten minutes and yet she had found time to change her clothes, to muss up her hair and, in a word, to revert to the way she had looked on board the *Southern Cross*, but to an even messier degree.

When she saw who it was, a flash of rage appeared in her brown eyes.

'What do you want with me? What are you doing here? This is my room! I'm paying for it and . . .'

She continued in a foreign language, probably Spanish, unscrewed the top off a bottle of eau de Cologne and poured most of the contents over her hands before dabbing her fevered brow with it.

'May I ask you a question?'

'I told them I didn't want to see anybody. Get out! Do you hear?'

She was walking around in her silk stockings. She was most likely not wearing garters, for they began to slide down her legs. One had already uncovered a podgy, very white knee.

'Why don't you go and put your questions to people who can give you the answers? But you don't dare, do you? Because he's a colonel. Because he's *Sir* Walter!

Don't you just love the *Sir*! Ha ha! If I told you only half of what I know . . .

'Look at this!'

She rummaged feverishly in her handbag and produced five crumpled 1,000-franc notes.

'This is what he just gave me! For what? For two years, for the two years that I've been living with him! That . . .'

She threw the notes on the carpet then, changing her mind, picked them up again and put them back in her bag.

'Of course, he promised he'd send me a cheque. But everybody knows what his promises are worth. A cheque! He won't even have enough money to get him to Porquerolles . . . though that won't stop him getting drunk on whisky every day!'

She wasn't crying, but there were tears in her voice. There was something unnerving about the distress exhibited by this woman who, when Maigret had seen her previously, had always seemed steeped in blissful sloth, supine in a hothouse atmosphere.

'And his precious Vladimir's just the same! He tried to kiss my hand and had the cheek to say: "It's adieu, madame, not au revoir."

'By God, they've got a nerve . . . But when the colonel wasn't around, Vladimir . . .

'But it's none of your business! Why are you still here? What are you waiting for? Are you hoping I'm going to tell you something?'

'Not at all!'

'But you can't deny that I'd be perfectly within my rights if I did . . .'

She was still walking up and down agitatedly, taking things out of her case, putting them down somewhere then a moment later picking them up again and putting them somewhere else.

'Leaving me at Épernay! In that disgusting hole, where it never stops raining! I begged him at least to take me to Nice, where I have friends. It was on his account that I left them.'

'Still, I should be glad they didn't kill me.'

'I won't talk! Got that? Why don't you clear off! Policemen make me sick! As sick as the English! If you're man enough, why don't you go and arrest him?'

'But you wouldn't dare! I know all about how these things work . . .'

'Poor Mary! She'll be called all sorts now. Of course, she had her bad side and she'd have done anything for Willy. Me, I couldn't stand him.'

'But to finish up dead like that . . .'

'Have they gone? . . . So who are you going to arrest, then? Maybe me?'

'Well, you just listen. I'll tell you something. Just one thing and you can make of it whatever you like. This morning, when he was getting dressed to appear before that magistrate – because he's forever trying to impress people and flashing his badges and medals – when he was dressing, Walter told Vladimir, in Russian, because he thinks I don't understand Russian . . .'

She was now speaking so quickly that she ran out of breath, stumbled over her words and reverted to throwing in snatches of Spanish.

'He told him to try and find out where the *Providence* was. Are you with me? It's the barge that was tied up near us at Meaux.

'They want to catch up with it and they're afraid of me.

'I pretended I hadn't understood.

'But I know you'd never ever dare to . . .'

She stared at her disembowelled suitcases and then around the room, which in only a few minutes she had succeeded in turning into a mess and filling with her acrid perfume.

'I don't suppose you've got any cigarettes? What sort of hotel is this? I told them to bring some, and a bottle of kümmel.'

'When you were in Meaux, did you ever see the colonel talking to anybody from the *Providence*?'

'I never saw a thing. I never paid attention to any of that . . . All I heard was what he said this morning. Why otherwise would they be worrying about a barge? Does anybody know how Walter's first wife died in India? The second one divorced him, so she must have had her reasons.'

A waiter knocked at the door with the cigarettes and a bottle. Madame Negretti reached for the packet and then hurled it into the corridor yelling:

'I asked for Abdullahs!'

'But madame . . .'

She clasped her hands together in a gesture which seemed like the prelude to an imminent fit of hysterics and shrieked:

'Ah! . . . Of all the stupid . . . Ah!'

She turned to face Maigret, who was looking at her with interest, and screamed at him:

'What are you still doing here? I'm not saying any more! I don't know anything! I haven't said anything! Got that? I don't want to be bothered any more with this business! . . . It's bad enough knowing that I've wasted two years of my life in . . .'

As the waiter left, he gave the inspector a knowing wink. And while the young woman, now a bundle of frayed nerves, was throwing herself on to the bed, he too took his leave.

The baker was still parked in the street outside.

'Well? Didn't you arrest her?' he asked in a disappointed voice. 'I thought . . .'

Maigret had to walk all the way to the station before he could find a taxi to take him back to the stone bridge.

7. The Bent Pedal

When the inspector overtook the *Southern Cross*, whose wash left the reeds swaying long after it had passed, the colonel was still at the wheel, and Vladimir, in the bow, was coiling a rope.

Maigret waited for the yacht at Aigny lock. The boat entered it smoothly, and, when it was made fast, the Russian got off to take his papers to the lock-keeper and give him his tip.

The inspector approached him and said: 'This cap belongs to you, doesn't it?'

Vladimir examined the cap, which was now dirty and ragged, then looked up at him.

'Thank you,' he said after a moment and took the cap.

'Just a moment! Can you tell me where you lost it?'

The colonel had been watching them carefully, without showing the least trace of emotion.

'I dropped it in the water last night,' Vladimir explained. 'I was leaning over the stern with a boat hook, clearing weeds which had fouled the propeller. There was a barge behind us. The woman was kneeling in their dinghy, doing her washing. She fished out my cap, and I left it on the deck to dry.'

'So it was left out all night on the deck.'

'Yes. This morning I didn't notice it was gone.'

'Was it already as dirty as this yesterday?'

'No! When the woman on the barge fished it out she put it in her wash with the rest.'

The yacht was rising by degrees. The lock-keeper already had both hands on the handle of the upper sluice gate.

'If I remember correctly, the boat behind you was the *Providence*, wasn't it?'

'I think so. I haven't seen it today.'

Maigret turned away with a vague wave of his hand then walked to his bicycle, while the colonel, as inscrutable as ever, engaged the motor and nodded to him as he passed through the lock.

The inspector remained where he was for a while, watching the yacht leave, thinking, puzzled by the astonishing ease and speed with which things happened on board the *Southern Cross*.

The yacht went on its way without paying any attention to him. The most that happened was that the colonel, from the wheel, asked the Russian the occasional question. The Russian returned short answers.

'Has the *Providence* got very far?' asked Maigret.

'She's maybe in the reach above Juvigny, five kilometres from here. She don't go as fast as that beauty there.'

Maigret reached there a few minutes before the *Southern Cross*, and from a distance Vladimir must have seen him talking to the bargee's wife.

The details she gave were clear. The day before, while doing her washing, which she then hung out on a line stretched across the barge, where it could be seen ballooning in the wind, she had indeed rescued the Russian's cap. Later, the man had given her little boy two francs.

It was now four in the afternoon. The inspector got back on his bike, his head filled with a jumble of speculations. The gravel of the towpath crunched under the tyres. His wheels parted the grit into furrows.

When he got to Lock 9, Maigret had a good lead over the Englishman.

'Can you tell me where the *Providence* is at this moment?'

'Not far off Vitry-le-François . . . They're making good time. They've got a good pair of horses and especially a carter who is no slouch.'

'Did they look as if they were in a hurry?'

'No more or less than usual. Oh, everybody's always in a hurry on the canal. You never know what might happen next. You can be held up for hours at a lock or go through in ten minutes. And the faster you travel the more money you earn.'

'Did you hear anything unusual last night?'

'No, nothing. Why? What happened?'

Maigret left without answering and from now on stopped at every lock, every boat.

He'd had no trouble making his mind up about Gloria Negretti. Though she'd done her level best to avoid saying anything damaging about the colonel, she had told everything she knew.

She was incapable of holding back! And equally incapable of lying! Otherwise, she would have made up a much more complicated tale.

So she really had heard Sir Walter ask Vladimir to find out about the *Providence*.

The inspector had also started to take an interest in the barge which had come from Meaux on Sunday evening, just before Mary Lampson was murdered. It was wood-built and treated with pitch and tar. Why did the colonel want to catch up with it? What was the connection between the *Southern Cross* and the heavy barge which could not go faster than the slow pace set by two horses?

As Maigret rode along the canal through monotonous countryside, pushing down harder and harder on the pedals, he came up with a number of hypotheses. But they led to conclusions which were fragmentary or implausible.

But hadn't the matter of the three clues been cleared up by Madame Negretti's furious accusations?

Maigret tried a dozen times to piece together the movements of all concerned during the previous night, about which nothing was known, except for the fact that Willy was dead.

Each time he tried, he was left with a poor fit, a gap. He had the impression that there was a person missing who was not the colonel, nor the dead man, nor Vladimir.

And now the *Southern Cross* was on the trail of someone on board the *Providence*.

Someone obviously who was mixed up in recent events! Could it be assumed that this someone had had a hand in the second crime, that is, in the murder of Willy, as well as in the first?

A lot of ground can be covered quickly at night on a canal towpath, by a bike for example.

'Did you hear anything last night? Did you notice anything unusual on the *Providence* when it passed through?'

It was laborious, discouraging work, especially in the drizzling rain that fell out of the low clouds.

'No, nothing.'

The gap between Maigret and the *Southern Cross,* which lost a minimum of twenty minutes at each lock, grew wider. The inspector kept getting back on his bicycle with growing weariness and, as he pedalled through a deserted reach of the canal, stubbornly picked up the threads of his reasoning.

He had already covered forty kilometres when the lock-keeper at Sarry said, in answer to his question:

'My dog barked. I think something must have happened on the road. A rabbit running past, maybe? I just went back to sleep.'

'Any idea where the *Providence* stopped last night?'

The man did a calculation in his head.

'Hang on a minute. I wouldn't be surprised if she hadn't got as far as Pogny. The skipper wanted to be at Vitry-le-François tonight.'

Another two locks. Result: nothing! Maigret now had to follow the lock-keepers on to their gates, for the further he went the busier the traffic became. At Vésigneul, three boats were waiting their turn. At Pogny, there were five.

'Noises, no,' grumbled the man in charge of the lock there. 'But I'd like to know what swine had the nerve to use my bike!'

The inspector had time to wipe the sweat from his face

now that he had a glimpse of what looked like light at the end of the tunnel. He was breathing hard and was hot. He had just ridden fifty kilometres without once stopping for a beer.

'Where is your bike now?'

'Open the sluices, will you, François?' the lock-keeper shouted to a carter.

He led Maigret to his house. The outside door opened straight into the kitchen, where men from the boats were drinking white wine which was being poured by a woman who did not put her baby down.

'You're not going to report us, are you? Selling alcohol isn't allowed. But everybody does it. It's just to do people a good turn. Here we are.'

He pointed to a lean-to made of wooden boards clinging to one side of the house. It had no door.

'Here's the bike. It's the wife's. Can you imagine, the nearest grocer's is four kilometres from here? I'm always telling her to bring the bike in for the night. But she says it makes a mess in the house. But I'll say that whoever used it must be a rum sort. I would never have noticed it myself . . .

'But as a matter of fact, the day before yesterday, my nephew, who's a mechanic at Rheims, was here for the day. The chain was broken. He mended it and at the same time cleaned the bike and oiled it.

'Yesterday no one used it. Oh, and he'd put a new tyre on the back wheel.

'Well, this morning, it was clean, though it had rained all night. And you've seen all that mud on the towpath.

'But the left pedal is bent, and the tyre looks as if it's done at least a hundred kilometres.

'What do you make of it? The bike's been a fair old way, no question. And whoever brought it back took the trouble to clean it.'

'Which boats were moored hereabouts?'

'Let me see . . . The *Madeleine* must have gone to La Chaussée, where the skipper's brother-in-law runs a bistro. The *Miséricorde* was tied up here, under the lock . . .'

'On its way from Dizy?'

'No, she's going downstream. Came from the Saône. I think there was just the *Providence*. She passed through last night around seven. Went on to Omey, two kilometres further along. There's good mooring there.'

'Do you have another bike?'

'No. But this one is still rideable.'

'No it isn't. You're going to have to lock it up somewhere. Hire another one if you need to. Can I count on you?'

The barge men were coming out of the kitchen. One of them called to the lock-keeper.

'Deserting your mates, Désiré?'

'Half a tick, I'm with this gentleman.'

'Where do you think I can catch up with the *Providence*?'

'Lemme see. She'll still be making pretty good time. I'd be surprised if you'd be up with her before Vitry.'

Maigret was about to leave. But he turned, came back, took a spanner from his tool bag and removed both pedals from the lock-keeper's wife's bicycle.

As he set off, the pedals he had pushed into his pockets made two unsightly bulges in his jacket.

The lock-keeper at Dizy had said to him jokingly:

'When it's dry everywhere else, there are at least two places where you can be sure of seeing rain: here and Vitry-le-François.'

Maigret was now getting near Vitry, and it was starting to rain again, a fine, lazy, never-ending drizzle.

The look of the canal was now changing. Factories appeared on both banks, and the inspector rode for some time through a swarm of mill girls emerging from one of them.

There were boats almost everywhere, some being unloaded, while others, which were lying up having their bilges emptied, were waiting.

And here again were the small houses which marked the outskirts of a town, with rabbit hutches made from old packing-cases and pitiful gardens.

Every kilometre there was a cement works or a quarry or a lime kiln. The rain mixed the white powder drifting in the air into the mud of the towpath. The cement dust left a film on everything, on the tiled roofs, the apple trees and the grass.

Maigret had started to weave right to left and left to right the way tired cyclists do. He was thinking thoughts, but not joined-up thoughts. He was putting ideas together in such ways that they could not be linked to make a solid picture.

When he at last saw the lock at Vitry-le-François, the growing dusk was flecked with the white navigation lights of a string of maybe sixty boats lined up in Indian file.

Some were overtaking others, some were hove to broadside on. When barges came from the opposite direction, the crew members exchanged shouts, curses and snippets of news as they passed.

'Ahoy, there, *Simoun*! Your sister-in-law, who was at Chalon-sur-Saône, says she'll catch up with you on the Burgundy canal . . . They'll hold back the christening . . . Pierre says all the best!'

By the lock gates a dozen figures were moving about busily.

And above it all hung a bluish, rain-filled mist, and through it could be seen the shapes of horses which had halted and men going from one boat to another.

Maigret read the names on the sterns of the boats. One voice called to him:

'Hello, inspector!'

It was a moment or two before he recognized the master of the *Éco-III*.

'Got your problem sorted?'

'It was something and nothing! My mate's a dimwit. The mechanic, who came all the way from Rheims, fixed it in five minutes.'

'You haven't seen the *Providence*, have you?'

'She's up ahead. But we'll be through before her. On account of the logjam, they'll be putting boats through the lock all tonight and maybe tomorrow night as well. Fact is there are at least sixty boats here, and more keep coming. As a rule, boats with engines have right of way and go before horse-boats. But this time, the powers that be have decided to let horse barges and motorized boats take turns.'

A friendly kind of man, with an open face, he pointed with one arm.

'There you go! Just opposite that crane. I recognize its white tiller.'

As he rode past the line of barges, he could make out people through open hatches eating by the yellow light of oil-lamps.

Maigret found the master of the *Providence* on the lock-side, arguing with other watermen.

'No way should there be special rules for boats with engines! Take the *Marie*, for example. We can gain a kilometre on her in a five-kilometre stretch. But what happens? With this priority system of theirs, she'll go through before us . . . Well, look who's here . . . it's the inspector!'

And the small man held out his hand, as if greeting a friend.

'Back with us again? The wife's on board. She'll be glad to see you. She said that, for a policeman, you're all right.'

In the dark, the ends of cigarettes glowed red, and the lights on the boats seemed so densely packed together that it was a mystery how they could move at all.

Maigret found the skipper's fat wife straining her soup. She wiped her hand on her apron before she held it out to him.

'Have you found the murderer?'

'Unfortunately no. But I came to ask a few more questions.'

'Sit down. Fancy a drop of something?'

'No thanks.'

'Go on, say yes! Look, in weather like this it can't do any harm. Don't tell me you've come from Dizy on a bike?'

'All the way from Dizy.'

'But it's sixty-eight kilometres!'

'Is your carter here?'

'He's most likely out on the lock, arguing. They want to take our turn. We can't let them push us around, not now. We've lost enough time already.'

'Does he own a bike?'

'Who, Jean? No!'

She laughed and, resuming her work, she explained:

'I can't see him getting on a bike, not with those little legs! My husband's got one. But he hasn't ridden a bike for over a year. Anyway I think the tyres have got punctures.'

'You spent last night at Omey?'

'That's right! We always try to stay in a place where I can buy my groceries. Because if, worse luck, you have to make a stop during the day, there are always boats that will pass you and get ahead.'

'What time did you get there?'

'Around this time of day. We go more by the sun than by clock time, if you follow me. Another little drop? It's gin. We bring some back from Belgium every trip.'

'Did you go to the shop?'

'Yes, while the men went for a drink. It must have been about eight when we went to bed.'

'Was Jean in the stable?'

'Where else would he have been? He's only happy when he's with his horses.'

'Did you hear any noises during the night?'

'Not a thing. At three, as usual, Jean came and made the coffee. It's our routine. Then we set off.'

'Did you notice anything unusual?'

'What sort of thing do you mean? Don't tell me you suspect poor old Jean? I know he can seem a bit, well, funny, when you don't know him. But he's been with us now for eight years, and I tell you, if he went, the *Providence* wouldn't be the same!'

'Does your husband sleep with you?'

She laughed again. And since Maigret was within range, she gave him a sharp dig in the ribs.

'Get away! Do we look as old as that?'

'Could I have a look inside the stable?'

'If you want. Take the lantern. It's on deck. The horses are still out because we're still hoping to go through tonight. Once we get to Vitry, we'll be fine. Most boats go down the Marne canal to the Rhine. It's a lot quieter on the run to the Saône – except for the culvert, which is eight kilometres long and always scares me stiff.'

Maigret made his way by himself towards the middle of the barge, where the stable loomed. Taking the storm lantern, which did service as a navigation light, he slipped quietly into Jean's private domain, which was full of a strong smell of horse manure and leather.

But his search was fruitless, though he squelched around in it for a quarter of an hour, during which time he could hear every word of what the skipper of the *Providence* was discussing on the wharf-side with the other men from the barges.

When a little while later he walked to the lock, where, to make up lost time, all hands were working together amid the screech of rusty crank-handles turning and the roar of roiling water, he spotted the carter at one of the gates, his horse whip coiled round his neck like a necklace, operating a sluice.

He was dressed as he had been at Dizy, in an old suit of ribbed corduroy and a faded slouch hat which had lost its band an age ago. A barge was emerging from the lock chamber, propelled by means of boat hooks because there was no other way of moving forward through the tangle of boats. The voices that called from one barge to another were rough and irritable, and the faces, lit at intervals by a navigation light, were deeply marked by fatigue.

All these people had been on the go since three or four in the morning and now had only one thought: a meal followed by a bed on to which they would at last be able to drop.

But they all wanted to be first through the congested lock so that they would be in the right place to start the next day's haul. The lock-keeper was everywhere, snatching up documents here and there as he passed through the crowd, dashing back to his office to sign and stamp them, and stuffing his tips into his pocket.

'Excuse me!'

Maigret had tapped the carter on the arm. The man turned slowly, stared with eyes that were hardly visible under his thicket of eyebrows.

'Have you got any other boots than the ones you've got on?'

Jean didn't seem to understand the words. His face wrinkled up even more. He stared at his feet in bewilderment.

Eventually he shook his head, removed his pipe from his mouth and muttered:

'Other boots?'

'Have you just got those, the ones you're wearing now?'

A yes, nodded very slowly.

'Can you ride a bike?'

A crowd started to gather, intrigued by their conversation.

'Come with me!' said Maigret. 'I want a word.'

The carter followed him back to the *Providence*, which was moored 200 metres away. As he walked past his horses, which stood, heads hanging, rumps glistening, he patted the nearest one on the neck.

'Come on board.'

The skipper, small and puny, bent double over a boat hook driven into the bottom of the canal, was pushing the vessel closer to the bank to allow a barge going downstream to pass.

He saw the two men step into the stable but had no time to wonder what was happening.

'Did you sleep here last night?'

A grunt that meant yes.

'All night? You didn't borrow a bike from the lockkeeper at Pogny, did you?'

The carter had the unhappy, cowering look of a simpleton who is being tormented or a dog which has always been well treated and then brutally thrashed for no good reason.

He raised one hand and pushed his hat back, scratching his head through his white mop, which grew as coarse as horse hair.

'Take off your boots.'

The man did not budge but looked out at the bank, where the legs of his horses were visible. One of them whinnied, as if it knew the carter was in some sort of trouble.

'Boots! And quick about it!'

And joining the action to the word, Maigret made Jean sit down on the plank which ran along the whole length of one wall of the stable.

Only then did the old man become amenable. Giving his tormentor a look of reproach, he set about removing one of his boots.

He was not wearing socks. Instead, strips of canvas steeped in tallow grease were wound round his feet and ankles, seeming to merge with his flesh.

The lantern shed only a dim light. The skipper, who had completed his manoeuvre, came forward and squatted on the deck so that he could see what was going on inside the stable.

While Jean, grumbling, scowling and bad-tempered, lifted his other leg, Maigret was using a handful of straw to clean the sole of the boot he held in his hand.

He took the left pedal from his pocket and held it against the boot.

A bemused old man staring at his bare feet made a strange sight. His trousers, which either had been made for a man even shorter than he was or had been altered, stopped not quite halfway down his calf.

And the strips of canvas greasy with tallow were blackish and pock-marked with wisps of straw and dirty sweepings.

Maigret stood close to the lantern and held the pedal, from which some of the metal teeth were missing, against faint marks on the leather.

'Last night, at Pogny, you took the lock-keeper's bike,' he said, making the accusation slowly, without taking his eyes off the two objects in his hands. 'How far did you ride?'

'Ahoy! *Providence*! . . . Move up! . . . The *Étourneau* is giving up its turn and will be spending the night here, in the lower reach.'

Jean turned and looked at the men who were now rushing about outside and then at the inspector.

'You can go and help get the boat through the lock,' said Maigret. 'Here! Put your boots on.'

The skipper was already pushing on his boat hook. His wife appeared:

'Jean! The horses! If we miss out turn . . .'

The carter had thrust his feet into his boots, was now on deck and was crooning in a strange voice:

'Hey! . . . Hey! . . . Hey up!'

The horses snorted and began moving forward. He jumped on to the bank, fell into step with them, treading heavily, his whip still wound round his shoulders.

'Hey! . . . Hey up!'

While her husband was heaving on the boat hook, the bargee's wife leaned on the tiller with all her weight to avoid colliding with a barge which was bearing down on them from the opposite direction, all that was visible of it being its rounded bows and the halo around its stern light.

The voice of the lock-keeper was heard shouting impatiently:

'Come on! ... Where's the *Providence*? ... What are you waiting for?'

The barge slid silently over the black water. But it bumped the lock wall three times before squeezing into the chamber and completely filling its width.

8. Ward 10

Normally, the four sluices of any lock are opened one after the other, gradually, to avoid creating a surge strong enough to break the boat's mooring ropes.

But sixty barges were waiting. Masters and mates whose turn was coming up helped with the operation, leaving the lock-keeper free to take care of the paperwork.

Maigret was on the side of the lock, holding his bicycle in one hand, watching the shadowy figures as they worked feverishly in the darkness. The two horses had continued on then stopped fifty metres further along from the upper gates, all by themselves. Jean was turning one of the crank handles.

The water rushed in, roaring like a torrent. It was visible, a foaming white presence, in the narrow gaps left vacant by the *Madeleine*.

But just as the cascading water was running most strongly, there was a muffled cry followed by a thud on the bow of the barge, which was followed by an unexplained commotion.

The inspector sensed rather than understood what was happening. The carter was no longer at his post, by the gate. Men were running along the walls. They were all shouting at the same time.

To light the scene there were only two lamps, one in the middle of the lift-bridge at the front of the lock and one on the barge, which was now rising rapidly in the chamber.

'Close the sluices!'

'Open the gates!'

Someone passed across an enormous boat hook, which caught Maigret a solid blow on the cheek.

Men from even distant boats came running. The lock-keeper came out of his house, shaking at the thought of his responsibilities.

'What's happened?'

'The old man . . .'

On each side of the barge, between its hull and the wall, there was less than a foot of clear water. This water, which came in torrents through the sluices, rushed down into those narrow channels then turned back on itself in a boiling mass.

Mistakes were made: for instance, when someone closed one sluice of the upper gate, which protested noisily and threatened to come off its hinges until the lock-keeper arrived to correct the error.

Only later was the inspector told that the whole lower stretch of canal could have been flooded and fifty barges damaged.

'Can you see him?'

'There's something dark. Down there!'

The barge was still rising, but more slowly now. Three sluices out of four had been closed. But the boat kept swinging, rubbing against the walls of the chamber and maybe crushing the carter.

'How deep is the water?'

'There's at least a metre under the boat.'

It was a horrible sight. In the faint light from the stable lamp, the bargee's wife could be seen running in all directions, holding a lifebuoy.

Visibly distressed, she was shouting:

'I don't think he can swim!'

Maigret heard a sober voice close by him say:

'Just as well! He won't have suffered as much . . .'

This went on for a quarter of an hour. Three times people thought they saw a body rising in the water. But boat hooks were directed to those places in the water, with no result.

The *Madeleine* moved slowly out of the lock, and one old carter muttered:

'I'll bet whatever you fancy that he's got caught under the tiller! I seen it happen once before, at Verdun.'

He was wrong. The barge had hardly come to a stop not fifty metres away before the men who were feeling all round the lower gates with a long pole shouted for help.

In the end, they had to use a dinghy. They could feel something in the water, about a metre down. And just as one man was about to dive in, while his tearful wife tried to stop him, a body suddenly burst on to the surface.

It was hauled out. A dozen hands grabbed for the badly torn corduroy jacket, which had been snagged on one of the gate's projecting bolts.

The rest unfolded like a nightmare. The telephone was heard ringing in the lock-keeper's house. A boy was despatched on a bicycle to fetch a doctor.

But it was no good. The body of the old carter was scarcely laid on the bank, motionless and seemingly lifeless, before a barge hand removed his jacket, knelt over the impressive chest of the drowned man and began applying traction to his tongue.

Someone had brought the lantern. The man's body seemed shorter, more thick-set than ever, and his face, dripping wet and streaked with sludge, had lost all colour.

'He moved! I tell you, he moved!'

There was no pushing or jostling. The silence was so intense that every word resounded as voices do in a cathedral. And underscoring it was the never-ending gush of water escaping through a badly closed sluice.

'How's he doing?' asked the lock-keeper as he returned.

'He moved. But not much.'

'Best get a mirror.'

The master of the *Madeleine* hurried away to get one from his boat. Sweat was pouring off the man applying artificial respiration, so someone else took over, and pulled even harder on the waterlogged man's tongue.

There was news that the doctor had arrived. He had come by car along a side road. By then, everyone could see old Jean's chest slowly rising and falling.

His jacket had been removed. His open shirt revealed a chest as hairy as a wild animal's. Under the right nipple was a long scar, and Maigret thought he could make out a kind of tattoo on his shoulder.

'Next boat!' shouted the lock-keeper, cupping both hands to his mouth. 'Look lively, there's nothing more you can do here.'

One bargee drifted regretfully away, calling to his wife, who had joined some other women a little further off in their commiserations.

'I hope at least that you didn't stop the engine?'

The doctor told the spectators to stand well back and scowled as he felt the man's chest.

'He's alive, isn't he?' said the first life-saver proudly.

'Police Judiciaire!' broke in Maigret. 'Is it serious?'

'Most of his ribs are crushed. He's alive all right, but I'd be surprised if he stays alive for very long! Did he get caught between two boats?'

'Most probably between a boat and the lock.'

'Feel here!'

The doctor made the inspector feel the left arm, which was broken in two places.

'Is there a stretcher?'

The injured man moaned feebly.

'All the same, I'm going to give him an injection. But get that stretcher ready as quick as you can. The hospital is 500 metres away . . .'

There was a stretcher at the lock. It was regulations. But it was in the attic, where the flame of a candle was observed through a skylight moving to and fro.

The mistress of the *Providence* stood sobbing some distance from Maigret. She was staring at him reproachfully.

There were ten men ready to carry the carter, who gave another groan. Then a lantern moved off in the direction of the main road, catching the group in a halo of light. A motorized barge, bright with green and red navigation lights, gave three whistles and moved off on its way to tie up at a berth in the middle of town, so that she would be the first to leave next morning.

Ward 10. It was by chance that Maigret saw the number. There were only two patients in it, one of whom was crying like a baby.

The inspector spent most of the time walking up and down the white-flagged corridor, where nurses ran by him, passing on instruction in hushed voices.

Ward 8, exactly opposite, was full of women who were talking about the new patient and assessing his chances.

'If they're putting him in Ward 10 . . .'

The doctor was plump and wore horn-rimmed glasses. He walked by two or three times in a white coat, without speaking to Maigret.

It was almost eleven when he finally stopped to have a word.

'Do you want to see him?'

It was a disconcerting sight. The inspector hardly recognized old Jean. He had been shaved so that two gashes, one on his cheek and the other on his forehead, could be treated.

He lay there, looking very clean in a white bed in the neutral glare of a frosted-glass lamp.

The doctor lifted the sheet.

'Take a look at this for a carcass! He's built like a bear. I don't think I ever saw a skeletal frame like it. How did he get in this state?'

'He fell off the lock gate just as the sluices were being opened.'

'I see. He must have been caught between the wall and

the barge. His chest is literally crushed in. The ribs just gave way.'

'And the rest?'

'My colleagues and I will examine him tomorrow, if he's still alive. We'll have to go carefully. One wrong move would kill him.'

'Has he regained consciousness?'

'No idea. That's perhaps the most surprising thing. A while back, as I was examining his cuts, I had the very clear impression that his eyes were half open and that he was watching me. But when I looked straight at him, he lowered his eyelids . . . He hasn't been delirious. All he does is groan from time to time.'

'His arm?'

'Not serious. The double fracture has already been reduced. But you can't put a whole chest back together the way you can a humerus. Where's he from?'

'I don't know.'

'I ask because he has some very strange tattoos. I've seen African Battalion tattoos, but they aren't like those. I'll show you tomorrow after they've removed the strapping so we can examine him.'

A porter came to say that there were visitors outside who were insisting on seeing the patient. Maigret himself went down to the porter's lodge, where he found the skipper and his wife from the *Providence*. They were in their Sunday best.

'We can see him, can't we, inspector? It's all your fault, you know. You upset him with all your questions. Is he better?'

'He's better. The doctors will tell us more tomorrow.'

'Let me see him. Just a peep round the door. He was such a part of the boat.'

She didn't say 'of the family' but 'of the boat', and was that not perhaps even more touching?

Her husband brought up the rear, keeping out of the way, ill at ease in a blue serge suit, his scrawny neck poking out of a detachable celluloid collar.

'I advise you not to make any noise.'

They both looked in at him, from the corridor. From there all they could see was a vague shape under a sheet, an ivory oval instead of a face, a lock of white hair.

The skipper's wife looked as if she was about to burst in at any moment.

'Listen, if we offered to pay, would he get better treatment?'

She didn't dare open her handbag there and then but she kept fidgeting with it.

'There are hospitals, aren't there, where if you pay? . . . The other patients haven't got anything catching, I hope?'

'Are you staying at Vitry?'

'We're not going home without him that's for sure! Blow the cargo! What time can we come tomorrow morning?'

'Ten o'clock!' broke in the doctor, who had been listening impatiently.

'Is there anything we can bring for him? A bottle of champagne? Spanish grapes?'

'We'll see he gets everything he needs.'

The doctor directed them towards the porter's lodge.

When she got there, the skipper's wife, who had a good heart, reached furtively into her handbag and pulled out a ten-franc note and slipped it into the hand of the porter, who looked at her in astonishment.

Maigret got to bed at midnight, after telegraphing Dizy with instructions to forward whatever communications might be sent to him there.

At the last moment, he'd learned that the *Southern Cross*, by overtaking most of the barges, had reached Vitry-le-François and was moored at the end of the queue of waiting boats.

The inspector had found a room at the Hotel de la Marne in town. It was a fair way from the canal. There he was free of the atmosphere he had lived in for the last few days.

A number of guests, all commercial travellers, sat playing cards.

One of them, who had arrived after the others, said:

'Seems like someone got drowned in the lock.'

'Want to make a fourth? Lamperrière's losing hand over fist. The man's dead, is he?'

'Don't know.'

And that was all. The landlady dozed by the till. The waiter scattered sawdust on the floor and, last thing, banked up the stove for the night.

There was a bathroom, just one. The bath had lost areas of its enamel. Even so, next morning at eight, Maigret used it, and then sent the waiter out to buy him a new shirt and collar.

But as the time wore on, he grew impatient. He was

anxious to get back to the canal. Hearing a boat hooting, he asked:

'Was that for the lock?'

'No, the lift-bridge. There are three in town.'

The sky was overcast. The wind had got up. He could not find the way back to the hospital and had to ask several people, because all roads invariably led him back to the market square.

The hospital porter recognized him. As he walked out to meet him, he said:

'Who'd have believed it? I ask you!'

'What? Is he alive? Dead?'

'What? You haven't heard? The super's just phoned your hotel . . .'

'Out with it!'

'Gone! Flown the coop! The doctor reckons it's not possible, says he can't have gone a hundred metres in the state he was in . . . Maybe, but the fact is he's not here!'

The inspector heard voices coming from the garden at the rear of the building and hurried off towards the sound.

There he found an old man he had never seen before. It was the hospital superintendent, and he was speaking sternly to the doctor from the previous evening and a nurse with ginger hair.

'I swear! . . .' the doctor said several times. 'You know as well as I do what it's like . . . When I say ten broken ribs that's very likely an underestimate . . . And that's leaving aside the effects of submersion, concussion . . .'

'How did he get out?' asked Maigret.

He was shown a window almost two metres above ground level. In the soil underneath it were the prints of two bare feet and a large scuff mark which suggested that the carter had fallen flat on the ground as he landed.

'There! The nurse, Mademoiselle Berthe, spent all night on the duty desk, as usual. She didn't hear anything. Around three o'clock she had to attend to a patient in Ward 8 and looked in on Ward 10. All the lights were out. It was all quiet. She can't say whether the man was still in his bed.'

'How about the other two patients?'

'There's one who's got to be trepanned. It's urgent. We're waiting now for the surgeon. The other one slept through.'

Maigret's eyes followed the trail, which led to a flower-bed where a small rose bush had been flattened.

'Do the front gates stay open at night?'

'This isn't a prison!' snapped the superintendent. 'How are we supposed to know if a patient is going to jump out of the window? Only the main door to the building was locked, as it always is.'

There was no point in looking for footprints or any other tracks. For the area was paved. In the gap between two houses, the double row of trees lining the canal was visible.

'To be perfectly frank,' added the doctor, 'I was pretty sure we'd find him dead this morning. Once it was clear there was nothing more we could try ... that's when I decided to put him in Ward 10.'

He was belligerent now, for the criticisms the super-intendent had directed at him still rankled.

For a while, Maigret circled the garden, like a circus

horse, then suddenly, signalling his departure by tugging the brim of his bowler, he strode away in the direction of the lock.

The *Southern Cross* was just entering the chamber. Vladimir, with the skill of an experienced sailor, looped a mooring rope over a bollard with one throw and stopped the boat dead.

Meanwhile, the colonel, wearing a long oilskin coat and his white cap, stood impassively at the small wheel.

'Ready the gates!' cried the lock-keeper.

There were now no more than twenty boats to be got through.

Maigret pointed to the yacht and asked: 'Is it their turn?'

'It is and it isn't. If you class her as a motorboat, then she has right of way over horse-drawn boats. But as she's a pleasure boat . . . Truth is, so few of them pass this way that we don't go much by the regulations. Still, since they saw the bargees right . . .'

The bargees in question were now operating the sluices.

'And the *Providence*?'

'She was holding everything up. This morning she went and moored a hundred metres further along, at the bend this side of the second bridge. Any news of the old feller? This business could set me back a pretty penny. But I'd like to see you try it! Officially, I'm supposed to lock them all myself. If I did that, there'd be a hundred of them queuing up every day. Four gates! Sixteen sluices! And do you know how much I get paid?'

He was called away briefly when Vladimir came to him with his papers and the tip.

Maigret made the most of the interruption to set off along the canal bank. At the bend he saw the *Providence*, which by now he could have picked out from any distance among a hundred barges.

A few curls of smoke rose from the chimney. There was no one about on deck. All hatches and doors were closed.

He almost walked up the aft plank which gave access to the crew's quarters.

But he changed his mind and instead went on board by the wide gangway which was used for taking the horses on and off.

One of the wooden panels over the stable had been slid open. The head of one of the horses showed above it, sniffing the wind.

Maigret looked down through it and made out a dark shape lying on straw. And close by, the skipper's wife was crouching with a bowl of coffee in one hand.

Her manner was motherly and oddly gentle. She murmured:

'Come on, Jean! Drink it up while it's hot. It'll do you good, silly old fool! Want me to raise your head up?'

But the man lying by her side did not move. He was looking up at the sky.

And against the sky Maigret's head stood out. The man must have seen him.

The inspector had the impression that on that face latticed with strips of sticking plaster there lurked a contented, ironic, even pugnacious smile.

The old carter tried to raise one hand to push away the

cup which the woman was holding close to his lips. But it fell back again weakly, gnarled, calloused, spotted with small blue dots which must have been the vestiges of old tattoos.

9. The Doctor

'See? He's come back to his burrow. Dragged himself, like an injured dog.'

Did the skipper's wife realize how seriously ill the man was?

Either way, she did not seem to be unduly concerned. She was as calm as if she were caring for a child with 'flu.

'Coffee won't do him any harm, will it? But he won't take anything. It must have been four in the morning when me and my husband were woken up by a lot of noise on board . . . I got the revolver and told him to follow me with the lantern.

'Believe it or not, it was Jean, more or less the way he is now . . . He must have fallen down in here from the deck . . . It's almost two metres.

'At first, we couldn't see very well. For a moment, I thought he was dead.

'My husband wanted to call the neighbours, to help us carry him and lie him down on a bed. But Jean twigged. He started gripping my hand, and did he squeeze! It was like he was hanging on to me for dear life!

'And I saw he was starting to, well, whimper.

'I knew what he was saying. Because he's been with us for eight years, you know. He can't speak. But I think he understands what I say to him. Isn't that right, Jean? Does it hurt?'

It was difficult to know whether the injured man's eyes were bright with intelligence or fever.

She removed a wisp of straw which was touching the man's ear.

'My life, you know, is my home, my pots and pans, my sticks of furniture. I think that if they gave me a palace to live in, I'd be as miserable as sin living in it.

'Jean's life is his stable . . . and his horses! Of course, there's always days, you know, when we don't move because we're unloading. Jean don't have any part in that. So he could go off to some bar.

'But no! He comes back and lies down, just here. He makes sure that the sun can get in . . .'

In his mind, Maigret imagined himself stretched out where the carter was lying, saw the pitch-covered wall on his right, the whip hanging from one twisted nail, the tin cup on another, a patch of sky through the hatch overhead and, to the right, the well-muscled hindquarters of the horses.

The whole place exuded animal warmth, a dense, many-layered vitality which caught the throat like the sharp-tasting wines produced by certain slopes.

'Will it be all right to leave him here, do you think?'

She motioned the inspector to join her outside. The lock was working at the same rate as the evening before. All around were the streets of the town, which were filled with a bustle that was alien to the canal.

'He's going to die, though, isn't he? What's he done?

You can tell me. I couldn't say anything before, could I? For a start I don't know anything. Once, just once, my husband saw him with his shirt off when he wasn't looking. He saw the tattoos. They weren't like the ones some sailors have done. We thought the same thing as you would have . . .

'I think it made me even fonder of him for it. I told myself he couldn't be what he seemed, that he was on the run . . .

'I wouldn't have asked him about it for all the money in the world. You surely don't think it was him that killed that woman? If you do, listen: if he did do it, I'd say she asked for it!

'Jean is . . .'

She searched for the word that expressed her thought. It did not come.

'Right! I can hear my husband getting up. I packed him off back to bed. He's always had a weak chest. Do you think that if I made him some strong broth . . .'

'The doctors will be on their way. Meanwhile, maybe it would be best to . . .'

'Do they really have to come? They'll hurt him and spoil his last moments, which . . .'

'It cannot be avoided.'

'But he's so comfortable here with us! Can I leave you here for a minute? You won't bother him again, will you?'

Maigret gave a reassuring nod of his head, went back inside the stable and from his pocket took a small tin. It contained a pad impregnated with viscous black ink.

He still could not tell if the carter was fully conscious.

His eyes were half open. The look in them was blank, calm.

But when the inspector lifted his right hand and pressed each finger one after the other against the pad, he had a split-second impression that the shadow of a smile flickered over his face.

He took the fingerprints on a sheet of paper, watched the dying man for a moment, as though he were expecting something to happen, looked one last time at the wooden walls and the rumps of the horses which were growing restive and impatient, then went outside.

Near the tiller, the bargee and his wife were drinking their morning *café au lait* fortified with dunked bread. They were looking his way. The *Southern Cross* was moored less than five metres from the *Providence*. There was no one on deck.

The previous evening, Maigret had left his bicycle at the lock. It was still there. Ten minutes later he was at the police station. He despatched an officer on a motorcycle to Épernay with instructions to transmit the fingerprints to Paris by belinograph.

When he was back on board the *Providence*, he had with him two doctors from the hospital with whom he had a difference of opinion.

The medics wanted their patient back. The skipper's wife was alarmed and looked pleadingly at Maigret.

'Do you think you can pull him through?'

'No. His chest has been crushed. One rib has pierced his right lung.'

'How long will he live for?'

'Most people would be dead already! An hour, maybe five . . .'

'Then let him be!'

The old man had not moved, had not even winced. As Maigret passed in front of the wife of the skipper, she touched his hand, shyly, her way of showing her gratitude.

The doctors walked down the gangplank, looking very unhappy.

'Leaving him to die in a stable!' grumbled one.

'Yes, but they also let him live in one . . .'

Even so, the inspector posted a uniformed officer near the barge and the yacht, with orders to inform him if anything happened.

From the lock he phoned the Café de la Marine at Dizy, where he was told that Inspector Lucas had just passed through and that he had hired a car at Épernay to drive him to Vitry-le-François.

Then there was a good hour when nothing happened. The master of the *Providence* used the time to apply a coat of tar to the dinghy he towed behind the barge. Vladimir polished the brasses on the *Southern Cross*.

Meanwhile the skipper's wife was constantly on deck, toing and froing between the galley and the stable. Once, she was observed carrying a dazzlingly white pillow. Another time it was a bowl of steaming liquid, doubtless the broth which she had insisted on making.

Around eleven, Lucas arrived at the Hotel de la Marne, where Maigret was waiting for him.

'How's things, Lucas?'

'Good. You look tired, sir.'

'What did you find out?'

'Not a lot. At Meaux, I learned nothing except that the yacht caused a bit of a rumpus. The barge men couldn't sleep for all the music and singing and they were talking of smashing the yacht up.'

'Was the *Providence* there?'

'It loaded not twenty metres from the *Southern Cross*. But nobody noticed anything unusual.'

'And in Paris?'

'I saw the two girls again. They admitted it wasn't Mary Lampson who gave them the necklace but Willy Marco. I had it confirmed in the hotel, where they recognized his photo, but no one had seen Mary Lampson. I'm not sure but I think Lia Lauwenstein was closer to Willy than she's letting on and that she'd already been helping him in Nice.'

'And Moulins?'

'Not a thing. I went to see the baker's wife. She really is the only Marie Dupin in the whole area. A nice woman, straight as a die. She doesn't understand what's been happening and is worried that this business is not going to do her any good. The copy of the birth certificate was issued eight years ago. There's been a new clerk in the registry for the last three years, and the previous one died last year. They trawled through the archives but didn't come up with anything involving this particular document.'

After a silence, Lucas asked:

'How about you?'

'I don't know yet. Maybe nothing, maybe the jackpot.

It could go one way or the other at any time. What are they saying at Dizy?'

'They reckon that if the *Southern Cross* hadn't been a yacht it wouldn't have been allowed to leave. There's also talk that the colonel has been married before.'

Saying nothing, Maigret led Lucas through the streets of the small town to the telegraph office.

'Give me Criminal Records in Paris.'

The belinogram with the carter's fingerprints should have reached the Prefecture two hours ago. After that, it was a matter of luck. Among 80,000 other sets, a match might be found straightaway, or it might take many hours.

'Listen with the earpiece, Lucas . . . Hello? . . . Who is this? . . . Is that you, Benoît? . . . Maigret here . . . Did you get the telephotograph I sent? . . . What's that? . . . You did the search yourself? . . . Just a moment.'

He left the call-booth and went up to the Post Office counter.

'I may need to stay on the line for quite some time. So please make absolutely sure I'm not cut off.'

When he picked up the receiver again, there was a gleam in his eye.

'Sit down, Benoît. You're going to give me everything in the files. Lucas is standing here next to me. He'll take notes. Go ahead . . .'

In his mind's eye, he could see his informant as clearly as if he had been standing next to him, for he was familiar with the offices located high in the attics of the Palais de Justice, where metal cabinets hold files on all the convicted felons in France and a good number of foreign-born gang-sters.

'First, what's his name?'

'Jean-Évariste Darchambaux, born Boulogne, now aged fifty-five.'

Automatically Maigret tried to recall a case featuring the name, but already Benoît, pronouncing every syllable distinctly, had resumed, and Lucas was busy scribbling.

'Doctor of medicine. Married a Céline Mornet, at Étampes. Moved to Toulouse, where he'd been a student. Then he moved around a lot ... Still there, inspector?'

'Still here. Carry on ...'

'I've got the complete file, for the record card doesn't say much ... The couple are soon up to their eyes in debt. Two years after he married, at twenty-seven, Darcham-baux is accused of poisoning his aunt, Julia Darchambaux, who had come to live with them in Toulouse and disap-proved of the kind of life he led. The aunt was pretty well off. The Darchambaux were her sole heirs.

'Inquiries lasted eight months, for no formal proof of guilt was ever found. Or at least the accused claimed – and some experts agreed with him – that the drugs prescribed for the old woman were not themselves harm-ful and that their use was an ambitious if extreme form of treatment.

'There was a lot of controversy ... You don't want me to read out the reports, do you?

'The trial was stormy, and the judge had to clear the court several times. Most people thought he should be acquitted, especially after the doctor's wife had given evidence. She stood up and swore that her husband was innocent and that if he was sent to a penal settlement in the colonies, she would follow him there.'

'Was he found guilty?'

'Sentenced to fifteen years' hard labour . . . Now, don't hang up! That's everything in our files. But I sent an officer on a bike round to the Ministry of the Interior . . . He's just got back.'

He could be heard speaking to someone standing behind him, and then there was a sound of papers being shuffled.

'Here we are! But it doesn't amount to much. The governor of Saint-Laurent-du-Maroni in French Guiana wanted to give Darchambaux a job in one of the hospitals in the colony . . . He turned it down . . . good record . . . "docile" prisoner . . . just one attempt to escape with fifteen others who had talked him into it.

'Five years later, a new governor undertook what he called the "rehabilitation" of Darchambaux. But almost immediately he noted in the margin of his report that there was nothing about the man he had interviewed to connect him with the professional man he once had been nor even to a man with a certain level of education.

'Right! Has that got your attention?

'He was given a job as an orderly at Saint-Laurent but he applied to be sent back to the colony.

'He was quiet, stubborn and spoke little. One of the medical staff took an interest in his case. He examined him from a mental health point of view but was unable to come up with a diagnosis.

'"There is," he wrote, underlining the words in red ink, "a kind of progressive loss of intellectual function proceeding in parallel with a hypertrophy of physical capacity."

'Darchambaux stole twice. Both times he stole food. On the second occasion he stole from another prisoner on the chain gang, who stabbed him in the chest with a sharpened flint.

'Journalists passing through advised him to apply for a pardon, but he never did,

'When his fifteen years were up, he stayed in the place to which he had been transported and found a manual job in a saw mill, where he looked after the horses.

'He was forty-five and had done his time. Thereafter, there is no trace of him.'

'Is that everything?'

'I can send you the file. I've only given you a summary.'

'Anything on his wife? You said she was born at Étampes, didn't you? Anyway, thanks for all that, Benoît. No need to send the details. What you've told me is enough.'

When, followed by Lucas, he stepped out of the phone box, he was perspiring profusely.

'I want you to phone the town hall at Étampes. If Céline Mornet is dead, you'll know, or at least you will if she died under that name. Also check with Moulins if Marie Dupin had any family living at Étampes.'

He walked through the town, looking neither to left nor right, hands deep in his pockets. He had to wait for five minutes at the canal because the lift-bridge was up, and a heavily laden barge was barely moving, its flat hull scouring the mud on the canal bed which rose to the surface in a mass of bubbles.

When he reached the *Providence*, he had a word with the uniformed man he had posted on the towpath.

'You can stand down . . .'

He saw the colonel pacing up and down on the deck of his yacht.

The skipper's wife hurried towards him looking more agitated than she had been earlier that morning. There were damp streaks on her cheeks.

'Oh, inspector, it's terrible!'

Maigret went pale, and his face turned grim.

'Is he dead?' he asked.

'No! Don't say such things! Just now I was with him, by myself. Because I should explain that though he liked my husband, he liked me better.

'I'm a lot younger than him. But despite that, he thought of me sort of as a mother.

'We'd go weeks without speaking. All the same . . . I'll give you an example. Most of the time my husband forgets my birthday, Saint Hortense's Day. Well, for the last eight years, Jean never went once without giving me flowers. Sometimes, we'd be travelling through the middle of open fields, and I'd wonder where he'd managed to get hold of flowers there.

'And on those days he'd always put rosettes on the horses' blinkers.

'Anyhow, I was sat by him, thinking it was probably his last hours. My husband wanted to let the horses out. They're not used to being cooped up for so long.

'I said no. Because I was sure it meant a lot to Jean to have them there too.

'I held his big hand.'

She was weeping now. But not sobbing. She went on talking through the large tears which rolled down her mottled cheeks.

'I don't know how things came to be like that ... I never had children myself. Though we'd always said we'd adopt when we reached the legal age.

'I told him it was nothing, that he'd get better, that we'd try to get a load for Alsace, where the country-side's a picture in summer.

'I felt his fingers squeezing mine. I couldn't tell him he was hurting me.

'It was then he started to talk.

'Can you understand it? A man like that who only yes-terday was as strong as his horses. He opened his mouth, straining so much that the veins on the sides of his head went all purple and swelled up.

'I heard this growly sound, like an animal's cry it was.

'I told him to stay quiet. But he wouldn't listen. He sat up on the straw, how I'll never know. And he still kept opening his mouth.

'Blood came out of it and dribbled down his chin.

'I wanted to call my husband, but Jean was still holding me tight. He was frightening me.

'You can't imagine what it was like. I tried to understand. I asked: "You want something to drink? No? Want me to fetch somebody?"

'He was so frustrated that he couldn't say anything! I

should have guessed what he meant. I did try.

'What do you reckon? What was he trying to ask me? And then it was as if something in his throat had burst, though it's no good asking me what. But he had a haemorrhage. In the end he lay down again, his mouth closed now, and on his broken arm too. It must have hurt like the very devil, but you wouldn't have thought he could feel anything.

'He just stared straight in front of him.

'I'd give anything to know what would make him happy before . . . before it's too late.'

Maigret walked to the stable in silence. He looked in through the open panel.

It was a sight as arresting, as unforgiving as watching the death of an animal with which there is no means of communicating.

The carter had curled up. He had partly torn away the strapping which the night doctor had placed around his torso.

Maigret could hear the faint, infrequent whispers of his breathing.

One of the horses had caught a hoof in its tether, but it stood absolutely still, as if it sensed that something grave was happening.

Maigret also hesitated. He thought of the dead woman buried under the straw of the stable at Dizy, then of Willy's corpse floating in the canal and the men, in the cold of early morning, trying to haul him in with a boat hook.

One hand played with the Yacht Club de France badge in his pocket.

He also recalled the way the colonel had bowed to the examining magistrate and requested permission to go on his way in a toneless, cool voice.

In the mortuary at Épernay, in an icy room lined with metal drawers, like the vaults of a bank, two bodies lay waiting, each in a numbered box.

And in Paris, two young women with badly applied make-up wandered from bar to bar, dogged by their gnawing fears.

Then Lucas appeared.

'Well?' cried Maigret, when he was still some way off.

'There has been no sign of life from Céline Mornet at Étampes since the day she requested the papers she needed for her marriage to Darchambaux.'

The inspector gave Lucas an odd look.

'What's up?' said Lucas.

'Sh!'

Lucas looked all round him. He saw no one, nothing that might give cause for alarm.

Then Maigret led him to the open stable hatch and pointed to the prone figure on the straw.

The skipper's wife wondered what they were going to do. From a motorized vessel chugging past, a cheerful voice shouted:

'Everything all right? Broken down?'

She started crying again, though she couldn't have said why. Her husband clambered back on board, carrying the tar bucket in one hand and a brush in the other, and called from the stern:

'There's something burning on the stove!'

She went back to the galley in a daze. Maigret said to Lucas, almost reluctantly:

'Let's go in.'

One of the horses snickered quietly. The carter did not move.

The inspector had taken the photo of the dead woman from his wallet, but he did not look at it.

10. *The Two Husbands*

'Listen, Darchambaux.'

Maigret was standing over the carter of the *Providence* when he spoke the words, his eyes never leaving the man's face. His mind elsewhere, he had taken his pipe out of his pocket but made no attempt to fill it.

Had he got the reaction he had expected? Whether it was or not, he sat down heavily on the bench fixed to the stable wall, leaned forward, cupped his chin in both hands and went on in a different voice.

'Listen. No need to get upset. I know you can't talk.'

A shadow appearing unexpectedly on the straw made him look up. He saw the colonel standing on the deck of the barge, by the open hatch.

The Englishman did not move. He went on watching what was happening from above, his feet higher than the heads of all three men below.

Lucas stood to one side in so far as he could, given the restricted size of the stable. Maigret, more on edge now, went on:

'Nobody's going to take you away from here. Have you got that, Darchambaux? In a few moments, I shall leave. Madame Hortense will be here instead.'

It was a painful moment, though no one could have said

exactly why. Without intending to, Maigret was speaking almost as gently as the skipper's wife.

'But first you have to answer a few questions. You can answer by blinking. Several people might be charged and arrested at any time now. That's not what you want, is it? So I need you to confirm the facts.'

While he spoke, the inspector did not take his eyes off the man, wondering who it was he had before him, the erstwhile doctor, the dour convict, the slow-witted carter or the brutal murderer of Mary Lampson.

The cast of face was rough, and the features coarse. But wasn't there a new expression in those eyes which excluded any hint of irony?

A look of infinite sadness.

Twice Jean tried to speak. And twice there was a sound like an animal moan and beads of pink saliva appeared on the dying man's lips.

Maigret could still see the shadow of the colonel's legs.

'When you were sent out to the penal settlement, all that time ago, you believed your wife would keep her promise and follow you there . . . It was her you killed at Dizy!'

Not a flicker! Nothing! The face acquired a greyish tinge.

'She didn't come . . . and you lost heart. You tried to forget everything, even who and what you were!'

Maigret was speaking more quickly now, driven by his impatience. He wanted it to be over. And above all he was afraid of seeing Jean slip away from him before this sickening interview was finished.

'You came across her by chance. By then you had become someone else. It happened at Meaux. Didn't it?'

He had to wait a good few moments before the carter, unresisting now, said yes by closing his eyes.

The shadow of the legs shifted. The whole barge rocked gently as a motor vessel passed by.

'And she hadn't changed, had she? Pretty, a flirt, liked a good time! They were dancing on the deck of the yacht. At first you didn't think about killing her. Otherwise, you wouldn't have needed to move her to Dizy.'

Was it certain the dying man could still hear? Since he was lying on his back, he must surely be able to see the colonel just above his head? But there was no expression in his eyes. Or at least nothing anyone could make sense of.

'She had sworn she would follow you anywhere. You'd seen the inside of a penal settlement. You were living in a stable. And then you suddenly had the idea of taking her back, just as she was, with her jewels, her painted face and her pale-coloured dress, and making her share your straw mattress. That's how it was, Darchambaux, wasn't it?'

His eyes did not blink. But his chest heaved. There was another moan. In his corner, Lucas, who was finding it unbearable, changed position.

'That's it! I can feel it!' said Maigret, the words now coming faster, as if he was being rushed along by them. Face to face with the woman who had been his wife, Jean the carter, who had virtually forgotten Doctor Darchambaux, had begun to remember, and mists of the past rose to meet him. And a strange plan had started to take shape. Was it vengeance? Not really. More an obscure desire to bring down to his level the woman who had promised to be his for the rest of their lives.

'So Mary Lampson lived for three days, hidden on this horse-boat, almost of her own free will.

'Because she was afraid. Afraid of this spectre from her past, who she felt was capable of anything, who told her she had to go with him!

'And even more scared because she was aware of how badly she had behaved.

'So she came of her own volition. And you, Jean, you brought her corned beef and cheap red wine. You went to her two nights in a row, after two interminable days of driving the boat along the Marne.

'When you got to Dizy . . .'

Again the dying man tried to stir. But his strength was gone, and he fell back, limp, drained.

'. . . she must have rebelled. She could not endure that kind of life any more. In a moment of madness, you strangled her rather than allow her to let you down a second time. You dumped her body in the stable. Is that what happened?'

He had to repeat the question five times until finally the eyelids flickered.

'Yes,' they said with indifference.

There was a faint scuffle on deck. It was the colonel holding back the skipper's wife, who was trying to get closer. She did not resist, for she was cowed by his solemn manner.

'So it was back to the towpath, back again to your life on the canal. But you were worried. You were scared. For you were afraid of dying, Jean. Afraid of being transported again. Afraid of being sent back to the colonies. Afraid, unbearably afraid of having to leave your horses, the stable, the straw, the one small corner which had become your entire universe. So one night, you took the lock-keeper's bike. I asked you about it. You guessed I had my suspicions.

'You rode back to Dizy intending to do something, anything, that would put me off the scent.

'Is that right?'

Jean was now so absolutely still that he might well have been dead. The expression on his face was a complete blank. But his eyelids closed once again.

'When you got there, there were no lights on the *Southern Cross*. You could safely assume that everyone on board was asleep. On deck an American cap was drying. You took it. You went into the stable, to hide it under the straw. It was the best way of changing the whole course of the investigation and switching the focus to the people on the yacht.

'You weren't to know that Willy Marco was outside, alone. He saw you take the cap and followed you. He was waiting for you by the stable door, where he lost a cufflink.

'He was curious. So he followed you when you started back to the stone bridge, where you had left the bike.

'Did he say something? Or did you hear a noise behind you?

'There was a fight. You killed him with those strong hands, the same hands that strangled Mary Lampson. You dragged the body to the canal . . .

'Then you must have walked on, head down. On the towpath, you saw something shining, the YCF badge. You thought that since the badge belonged to someone you'd seen around, maybe you'd noticed it on the colonel's lapel, you left it at the spot where the fight had taken place. Answer me, Darchambaux. That was how it happened, wasn't it?'

'Ahoy, *Providence*! Got a problem?' called another barge captain, whose boat passed so close that his head could be seen gliding past level with the hatch.

But then something strange and troubling happened. Jean's eyes filled with tears. Then he blinked, very fast, as though he was confessing to everything, to get it over and done with once and for all. He heard the skipper's wife answering from the stern, where she was waiting:

'It's Jean! He's hurt himself!'

As Maigret got to his feet, he said:

'Last night, when I examined your boots, you knew that I would sooner or later get to the truth. You tried to kill yourself by jumping into the lock.'

But the carter was now so far gone and his breathing so laborious that the inspector did not even wait for a response. He nodded to Lucas and cast one last look around him.

A diagonal shaft of sunlight entered the stable, striking the carter's left ear and the hoof of one of the horses.

Just as the two men were leaving, not finding anything else to say, Jean tried again to speak, urgently, disregarding the pain. Wild-eyed, he half sat up on his straw.

Maigret paid no attention to the colonel, not immediately.

He crooked one finger and beckoned the woman, who was watching him from the stern.

'Well? How is he?' she asked.

'Stay by him.'

'Can I? And no one will come and . . .'

She did not dare finish. She had gone rigid when she heard the muffled cries uttered by Jean, who seemed frightened that he would be left to die alone.

Suddenly, she ran to the stable.

Vladimir sat on the yacht's capstan, a cigarette between his lips, wearing his white cap slantwise, splicing two rope ends.

A policeman in uniform was standing on the canal bank. From the barge Maigret called:

'What is it?'

'We've had the reply from Moulins.'

He handed over an envelope with a brief note which said:

Marie Dupin, wife of the baker, has confirmed that she had a distant cousin at Étampes named Céline Mornet.

Maigret stared hard at the colonel, sizing him up. He was wearing his white yachting cap with the large crest. His eyes were just starting to acquire the faintest blue-green tinge, which doubtless meant that he had consumed a relatively small quantity of whisky.

'You had suspicions about the *Providence*?' Maigret asked him point blank.

It was so obvious! Wouldn't Maigret also have concentrated on the barge if his suspicions had not been diverted momentarily to the people on the yacht?

'Why didn't you say anything?'

The reply was well up to the standard of Sir Walter's interview with the examining magistrate at Dizy.

'Because I wanted to take care of the matter myself.'

It was more than enough to express the contempt the colonel felt for the police.

'And my wife?' he added almost immediately.

'As you said yourself, and as Willy Marco also said, she was a charming lady.'

Maigret spoke without irony. But in fact he was more interested in the sounds coming from the stable than in this conversation.

Just audible was the faint murmur of a single voice. It belonged to the skipper's wife, who sounded as if she were comforting a sick child.

'When she married Darchambaux, she already had a taste for the finer things of life. It seems very likely that it was on her account that the struggling doctor he then was did away with his aunt. I'm not saying she aided and abetted him. I'm saying that he did it for her. And she knew it, which explains why she stood up in court and swore that she would follow him and be with him.

'A charming lady. Though that's not the same thing as saying she was a heroine.

'She loved life too much. I'm sure you can understand that, colonel.'

The mixture of sun, wind and threatening clouds

suggested a shower could break out at any moment. The light was shifting constantly.

'Not many people return from those penal settlements. She was pretty. All of life's pleasures were hers for the taking. There was only her name to hold her back. So when she got to the Côte d'Azur and met someone, her first admirer, who was ready to marry her, she got the idea of sending to Moulins for the birth certificate of a distant cousin she remembered.

'It's so easy to do! So easy that there's talk now of taking the fingerprints of newborn babies and adding them to the official registers of births.

'She got a divorce and then became your wife.

'A charming lady. No real harm in her, I'm sure. But she liked a good time, didn't she? She was in love with youth and love and the good things in life.

'And maybe sometimes the embers would be fanned and she'd feel the unaccountable need to go off and cut loose . . .

'Know what I think? I believe she went off with Jean not so much because of his threats but because she needed to be forgiven.

'The first day, hiding in the stable on board this boat, among the horsey smells, she must have derived some sort of satisfaction from the thought that she was atoning.

'It was the same thing as the time she vowed to the jury she would follow her husband to Guiana.

'Such charming creatures! Their first impulses are generous, if theatrical. They are so full of good intentions.

'It's just that life, with its betrayals, compromises and its overriding demands, is stronger.'

Maigret had spoken rather bitterly but had not stopped listening for sounds coming from the stable while simultaneously keeping a constant eye on the movement of boats entering and leaving the lock.

The colonel had been standing in front of him with his head bowed. When he looked up now it was with obviously warmer sentiments, even a touch of muted affection.

'Do you want a drink?' he said and pointed to his yacht.

Lucas had been standing slightly to one side.

'You'll keep me informed?' said the inspector, turning to him.

Between them, there was no need for explanations. Lucas had understood and began to prowl silently round the stable.

The *Southern Cross* was as ship-shape as if nothing had happened. There was not a speck of dust on the mahogany walls of the cabin.

In the middle of the table was a bottle of whisky, a siphon and glasses.

'Stay outside, Vladimir!'

Maigret looked round him with new eyes. He was not there now pursuing some fine sliver of truth. He was more relaxed, less curt.

And the colonel treated him as he had treated Monsieur Clairfontaine de Lagny.

'He's going to die, isn't he?'

'He could go at any time. He's known since yesterday.'

The sparkling soda water spurted from the siphon. Sir Walter said sombrely:

'Your good health!'

Maigret drank as greedily as his host.

'Why did he run away from the hospital?'

The rhythm of their conversation had slowed. Before answering, the inspector looked round him carefully, taking in every detail of the cabin.

'Because . . .'

As he felt for his words his host was already refilling their glasses.

'. . . a man with no ties, a man who has severed all links with his past, with the kind of man he used to be . . . a man like that has to have something to cling to! He had his stable . . . the smell of it . . . the horses . . . the coffee he drank scalding hot at three in the morning ahead of a day spent slogging along the towpath until it was evening . . . It was his burrow, if you like, his very own corner, a place filled with animal warmth.'

Maigret looked the colonel in the eye. He saw him turn his head away. Reaching for his glass he added:

'There are all kinds of bolt-holes. Some have the smell of whisky, eau de Cologne, a woman and the sounds of gramophone records . . .'

He stopped and drank. When he looked up again, his host had had time to empty a third glass.

Sir Walter watched him with his large, bleary eyes and held out the bottle.

'No thanks,' protested Maigret.

'Yes for me! I need it.'

Was there not a hint of affection in the look he gave the inspector?

'My wife . . . Willy . . .'

At that moment, a thought sharp as an arrow struck the inspector. Was not Sir Walter as alone, just as lost, as Jean, who was busy dying in his stable?

And at least the carter had his horses by him and his motherly Madame Hortense.

'Drink up! That's right! I'd like to ask . . . You're a gentleman . . .'

He spoke almost pleadingly. He held out his bottle rather shamefacedly. Vladimir could be heard moving about up on deck.

Maigret held out his glass. But there was a knock at the door. Through it came Lucas's voice:

'Inspector?'

And through the crack in the door he added:

'It's over.'

The colonel did not move. He watched grimly as the two policemen walked away.

When Maigret turned round, he saw him drink the glass he had just filled for his guest in one swallow. Then he heard him sing out:

'Vladimir!'

A number of people had gathered by the *Providence* because from the bank they had heard the sound of sobbing.

It was Hortense Canelle, the wife of the master, on her knees by Jean's side. She was talking to him even though he had been dead for several minutes.

Her husband was on deck, waiting for the inspector to

come. He hurried towards him with little skipping steps, thin as a wraith, visibly flustered, and said in a desperate voice:

'What shall I do? He's dead! My wife . . .'

An image which Maigret would never forget: the stable, seen from above, the two horses almost filling it, a body curled up with half its head buried in straw. And the fair hair of the skipper's wife catching all the sun's rays while she gently moaned and at intervals repeated:

'Oh Jean! Poor Jean!'

Exactly as if Jean had been a child and not this granite-hard old man, with a carcass like a gorilla, who had cheated all the doctors!

11. Right of Way

No one noticed, except Maigret.

Two hours after Jean died, while the body was being stretchered to a waiting vehicle, the colonel, his eyes bloodshot but as dignified as ever, asked:

'Do you think now they can issue the burial permit?'

'You'll get it tomorrow.'

Five minutes later, Vladimir, with his customary neat movements, cast off.

Two boats making towards Dizy were waiting to descend through the Vitry lock.

The first was already being poled towards the chamber when the yacht skimmed past it, skirted its rounded bow, and slipped ahead of it into the open lock.

There were shouts of protest. The skipper yelled to the lock-keeper, telling him it was his turn, that he'd be making a complaint and much more of the same.

But the colonel, wearing his white cap and officer's uniform, did not even turn round.

He was standing at the brass wheel, expressionless, looking dead ahead.

When the lock gates were closed, Vladimir jumped on to the lock-side, showed his papers and offered the traditional tip.

'For God's sake!' grumbled a carter. 'These yachts get

away with anything. All it takes is ten francs at every lock
. . .'

The stretch of canal below the Vitry-le-François lock was congested. It hardly seemed possible that anything could pole a way through all the boats waiting for their turn.

But the gates had barely opened when the water started churning around the propeller, and the colonel, with a perfunctory movement of his hand, let in the clutch.

The *Southern Cross* got up to full speed in a twinkling and flitted past the heavily laden barges despite the shouts and protests but did not so much as graze any of them.

Two minutes later, it vanished round the bend, and Maigret turned to Lucas, who was walking at his side:

'They're both dead drunk.'

No one had guessed. The colonel was a respectable gentleman with a large gold insignia on the front of his cap.

Vladimir, in his striped jersey, with his forage cap perched on his head, had not made one clumsy movement.

But if Sir Walter's apoplectic neck showed reddish-purple, his face was sickly pale, there were large bags under his eyes and his lips had no colour.

The smallest jolt would have knocked the Russian off balance, for he was asleep standing up.

On board the *Providence* everything was shut up, silent. Both horses were tethered to a tree a hundred metres from the barge.

The skipper and his wife had gone into town, to buy clothes for the funeral.